MAGIC OF THE GARGOYLES

GARGOYLE GUARDIAN CHRONICLES BOOK 1

REBECCA CHASTAIN

M
Y
M

Copyright © 2014 by Rebecca Chastain
Excerpt from *Curse of the Gargoyles* copyright © by Rebecca Chastain
Cover design by Yocla Designs

www.rebeccachastain.com

Mind Your Muse Books
PO Box 374
Rocklin, CA 95677

ISBN: 978-0-9992385-1-6

ALSO BY REBECCA CHASTAIN

THE MADISON FOX ADVENTURES

A Fistful of Evil

A Fistful of Fire

A Fistful of Frost (forthcoming)

GARGOYLE GUARDIAN CHRONICLES

Magic of the Gargoyles

Curse of the Gargoyles

Secret of the Gargoyles

Lured (a novelette)

STAND ALONE

Tiny Glitches (paranormal romance)

NEVER MISS ANY NOVEL NEWS:

Join Rebecca's newsletter to receive emails regarding future releases, bonus content, and behind-the-scenes information.

Visit RebeccaChastain.com

To Cody, who makes every day magical

ACKNOWLEDGMENTS

When I sat down to write *Magic of the Gargoyles*, I thought it would be a ten-page short story, sort of a palate cleanser between writing two novels. Instead, it grew into a tiny novel of its own, in a world ripe for adventure. The structure of a short story and a novella vary greatly, and this book went through many rewrites, left a lot of text on the editing room floor, and treated a few characters to Play-Doh-like remolding makeovers. Major alterations like these can blind me to smaller problems, so thank you to the many great authors at the Online Writing Workshop for Science Fiction, Fantasy and Horror for giving me so much valuable feedback. Also, thank you to my fantastic beta readers, Deb, Debbie, and Sara B., for your eagle eyes and helpful suggestions. Finally, thank you to Carrie Andrews and Amanda Zeier for giving the story its final editing polish.

I am endlessly grateful to my family for all your support. I know this story veered into darker territory than you prefer, Mom, but you read it anyway. At a time when I'd become numb to the story during rewrites, your response to the gargoyles' torture reminded me that greater evil doesn't always make a greater story. The rewrites were so much better because of it; thank you! Sara E., you are officially my most valiant beta reader; thank you for your invaluable feedback, as a reader and a sister. Is it too soon to ask if you're ready to read the next twelve iterations of my WIP?

Finally, Cody, thank you for your infinite patience, the time and space to write, and your perpetual support. You're a shining example for writers' spouses everywhere.

Constructive Elements

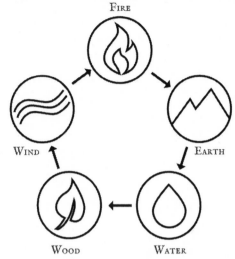

Destructive Elements

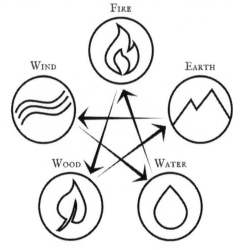

With one last twist of a filament of earth magic, I fused together the delicate seams of the quartz tube. Slumping forward, I braced my elbows on the table and rested my cheekbones on my palms, cupping my weary eyes in darkness. Six down, six finicky tubes to go. The specifications of this project taxed my substantial skills with quartz magic, which was the point. This project would launch my business and prove that even though I was only a midlevel earth elemental, my quartz skills were equal to or better than more powerful full-spectrum elementals. These fussy tubes would fund the down payment on the lease for the shop I coveted in the Pinnacle Pentagon Center. I could finally quit my demeaning job at Jones and Sons Quarry, be my own boss, and begin a career creating one-of-a-kind quartz master-pieces I could take pride in.

My entire future rested on these fragile vials, and they were due tomorrow at four.

Dull pain pounded my back muscles. Night had crept over the city while I worked, and my jerky movements as I stood and stretched were reflected in the semicircle of bay windows in front of my worktable. Purple smears of exhaustion beneath my eyes were exaggerated in the dark windows, and my pale face floated above a dirt-smeared navy shirt. I checked the clock: almost midnight. Sixteen hours until my deadline, and eight of those would be taken up by my Jones and Sons workday. There was no time for a break. If anything, I needed to work faster.

Groaning, I redid my ponytail, tucking shorter wisps of strawberry-blond hair behind my ears before giving my hard wooden chair the stink eye. Mentally chanting, *Pinnacle Pentagon*, to motivate myself, I reached for another seed crystal.

Frantic tapping shook the glass in the balcony door. I pulled the door open, knowing it was Kylie, my best friend and the tenant who shared my second-floor apartment balcony. "I really can't talk. I need to finish—"

"Help! Help! They've got—"

Something small and hard slammed into my stomach. I staggered backward into my chair and crashed to the floor. A small boulder skipped across the wooden floor and smashed into the wall.

"You're a human!"

I shrieked. The voice came from inside my room. I twisted, scrambling onto my bed.

Against the wall, the rock moved.

Beautiful blue dumortierite quartz veined with green aventurine twisted into a winged panther no bigger than a house cat. A pissed-off, solid-stone, magical, winged house cat. A gargoyle—no, a baby gargoyle. A hatchling.

Her eyes glowed feverishly. Long polished blue claws gouged into the floor when she launched into the air. Her agile stone wings unfolded with a soft gritty sound.

I lurched backward across the bed until I was pressed against the wall. The mattress shook when the hatchling pounced on the space I'd just vacated. Sharp claws bunched in my yellow bedspread. She raised her muzzle, mouth open, and sniffed the air.

I eased toward the foot of the bed, readying my escape into the hallway.

"It's you! Your magic smells so good. I thought—"

My magic has a smell?

The gargoyle's eyes darted to the open door, then back to me. She arched her stone back and hissed at me, the sound dying to a hair-raising growl. The tip of her stone tail slashed back and forth, gouging my wooden headboard.

"I need help."

"My help?" Gargoyles—even baby gargoyles—didn't interact with midlevel elementals like me, and they certainly didn't ask for our help. "There's a full-spectrum elemental just—" I started to point up the street but froze when she snarled at me.

"No other humans! Before it's too late." The gargoyle's words were smooth coming out of her rock throat, with just a hint of a lisp from her tongue working around enormous teeth.

I stared into her glowing blue eyes, seeing past the bared fangs and agitated movements, reading her fear for the first time. I reached for her, then pulled my hand back when she shied from me.

"Too late for what?"

"You can save him. Hurry!"

"Save him? Save who? If someone is hurt, I can send for a healer." Where were this gargoyle's parents?

"No. I need you." Large blue eyes implored me. "Please!"

A thousand reasons why I should find someone else to

help the gargoyle crowded my mind, but the hatchling's urgency was contagious. Someone was injured. I didn't want to waste time arguing with her, but was I really the best choice? I could work earth, but healing usually took someone talented with all five elements.

"Are you sure you don't want me to get—" *someone stronger?* I started to ask, but she cut me off with another sharp, "Please!"

Gargoyles were creatures without guile, and this baby was obviously terrified for someone's life. If she thought I could help, I had to try. I took a deep breath. "Okay. Let's go."

The gargoyle whirled and launched for the open doorway, moving with the silent fluidity of a flesh-and-blood panther.

"I'll take the stairs," I said. I snatched up my shoes and coat and raced to the door.

My studio apartment was one of four on the upper floor of a converted Victorian house. At midnight, everyone else in the house was asleep, just the way my landlady Ms. Josephine Zuberrie liked it.

As I sprinted down the stairs as quietly as possible, shoes in hand, I reviewed everything I knew about gargoyles. It wasn't much. Gargoyles favored those strongest in magic—full-spectrum pentacle potential, or FSPP, elementals. When they chose, they could enhance a person's magic, but I'd only heard of them doing so during large-scale rituals conducted by a five linked FSPPs. Despite being creatures of earth, they were not partial to any particular elemental magic; instead, they were attracted to a person's strength of earth, wood, air, water, or fire magic.

Which is why, as a midlevel earth elemental, this was the first time I'd spoken with a gargoyle.

I eased the front door shut and dropped my shoes to the

porch, wiggled my feet into them, and yanked the laces tight. When I spun around, the gargoyle dropped from the roof to the porch railing, almost clipping my head with a heavy rock wing. I swallowed a startled scream.

"Hurry," she trilled. With a squeal of protesting wood, followed by the crack of stone smashing into stone, the gargoyle leapt from the balcony to the sidewalk ten feet below. Wincing, I raced down the porch steps after her, praying to be out of sight before Ms. Zuberrie investigated the racket.

By the time I reached the sidewalk, the gargoyle had almost a block lead on me, moving unexpectedly fast for such a small creature made of stone. In wing-assisted leaps, she bounded into the darkness. I sprinted headlong down the center of the deserted street, chasing the sporadic glimpses of panther-shaped dumortierite in the puddles of lamplight. The baby gargoyle kept me in sight, but only just. My lungs and legs burned after the first five blocks. My vision tunneled to the broken asphalt and gargoyle in front of me. I didn't notice when the lamps ended, only that the dark blue gargoyle was harder to see, and by the time I did take in my surroundings, we were deep in the blight and I was lost.

2

The blight was the oldest part of the city, long since abandoned by the wealthy and middle class, left to crumble and rot, along with its impoverished residents. It was a seedbed for crime and a haven for the immoral. Doorways glowed with protection spells and menacing traps. Unseen eyes tracked me from the shadows.

Alarm skittered through my body, giving me fresh energy. Ms. Zuberrie's neighborhood was on the fringes of the blight—holding it at bay, according to my landlady—and her endless repertoire of blight tales gave me nightmares. To be here, at night, alone, was sheer insanity.

A high-pitched sound, like an animal being gutted alive, echoed through the hulking shadows of old warehouse buildings, setting my neck hair on end. I slowed, having lost sight of the gargoyle. Menacing shapes loomed in the darkness to either side of the desolate road. I identified each item as I jogged past—*empty trailer, rubble from a collapsed wall, enormous splintered wooden ward*—trying to reassure myself.

Someone rounded the far corner of the warehouse at a

sprint, coming right for me. There wasn't time to hide. I crouched, heart in throat. Before I could gather my magic, a wide-eyed, scrawny boy tore past me. He glanced once over his shoulder, but it wasn't at me. I watched until the darkness swallowed him, then turned with new dread back in the direction he had come—and the direction the gargoyle had disappeared.

Voices bounced off the warehouse walls, footsteps following. I sprinted for a pile of rusty barrels and crouched behind their bulk. Seconds later, a horse-size fireball blazed down the street, scorching the pavement and casting sinister light on the graffiti-crusted buildings. I tucked into a tight ball, shielding my face from the heat and my body from visibility.

The fire hit a stone wall at the end of the street and burned out. Blinded, I blinked to clear the flaming afterimage. Whooping and shouting reverberated off the metal walls.

"Enough! Save it for the splinter-heads."

I peeked between the barrels. Five guys rounded the corner, a dozen fist-size glowballs darting chaotically around their heads. Three men followed. No, more. A whole gang. They milled together less than ten feet from where I hid, body-slamming each other and loosing war cries, all caught up in the same high. In the dizzying, erratic light, I could make out two important details: Every single one of them was dressed in bright orange Fire Eater gang colors, and all of them were linked with a potent amplification spell.

Easing back on my heels, I curled into the tightest ball possible. Fire Eaters ruled half of the blight, and updates of the city guard's ongoing attempts to contain their violent acts were featured prominently in the headlines of the *Terra*

Haven Chronicle. From the size of that fireball and the amount of magic resonating among the men, I could predict tomorrow's feature story.

I didn't even think about touching my magic, fearing they would sense it. I didn't breathe. I maintained my cramped huddle until the men rounded the far bend in the street. Only then did I let out my breath and suck in a new one. I waited until I could no longer hear even an echo of their voices before I uncurled.

"Hurry!"

I jumped and clutched my heart. The gargoyle leapt from the rooftop above me and raced around the warehouse wall where the Fire Eaters had emerged. *I shouldn't be here,* I told myself. *This is a horrible, horrible mistake.* But I'd promised the baby gargoyle I'd help. I couldn't turn back now.

I rounded the corner and froze.

Moonlight bathed the expansive loading dock, illuminating an elaborate chalk pentagram the likes of which I'd never seen before. Someone had drawn five pentagrams, one atop the other, each skewed a few degrees so that every angle had five points. In the center was a small lump of rock. The dock was empty of people. The tiny gargoyle paced the edge of the mutated pentagram's circle.

I edged forward, squinting at the lump in the center of the pentagram. My toes kicked something small, sending it clanging into the warehouse's collapsed metal roof. I spun, checking my surroundings. I was still alone. I scanned the shadowed ground. Focus talismans—candles, rocks, glass, wooden carvings, crude fans—were scattered in every direction. There were enough for fifteen people, not the traditional five. If I hadn't just seen a mob of Fire Eaters with the power of linked FSPPs, I wouldn't have believed this mutated pentagram was anything other than graffiti.

I wove a standard five-element test sphere. It popped into existence in front of me, then flattened to a pentagram the size of my palm, each side glowing with the magic of its specific element. If any harmful magic remained, especially a trap, it would alert me before I blundered into it.

I floated the glowing pentagram safely across the chalk twice before I let the small star dissipate. I crept toward the lump. In the moonlight, it was impossible to make out its form. Kneeling, I grabbed fire, forming a ball of light. A small sun burst into existence above my head. I gawked.

Light was the most basic fire spell, one I used every day. My glowballs were never larger than my cupped hands—any bigger and they were too weak to produce light. Yet the sun above me was larger than my head, and I could see molten flames arc within it, twisting and turning hypnotically. It was like I'd jumped from mildly talented to FSPP.

"Impossible," I breathed. The chalk pentagram was bathed in daylight. Was this strange design the reason for my enhanced powers? Had the Fire Eaters' spell left charged fire elemental magic I couldn't detect within the circle?

The lump of rock moved. I stumbled backward, tripping and landing on my butt. The sun cast sharp shadows across the rock, the flickering fire within it making the rock look like it quivered. Slowing my breathing, I extinguished the sun and replaced it with a manageable ball of soft light, keeping an eye on the rock. When I realized what I was seeing, I scrambled forward again.

The rock opened its toucan-shaped mouth and released a high-pitched cry that wrenched my heart. The baby gargoyle didn't look to have the strength to lift its thick neck, and its long, spindly tail lay lifeless.

"Can you save him?"

I jumped, having forgotten all about the gargoyle panther. She pawed at the chalk circle, careful not to cross it.

My caution morphed to horror when I realized the significance of the hatchling's placement. Using a magical creature as a pentagram focus drained the creature of its own magic and its life. Rumors said the average magical creature doubled a person's power when used as a focus, but gargoyles were natural elemental enhancers when they chose; a scumbag who used a gargoyle as a focus would get a far greater boost. The idea was repulsive in theory, enraging in reality. It was black magic, punishable by nulli-fication.

I examined the injured gargoyle closer. Unlike the panther-shaped hatchling, this one's body was mostly rose quartz, with sporadic coils of blue dumortierite. Jagged patches marred his otherwise smooth sides, and his entire stomach looked like raw, unpolished crystal. Acting on instinct, I reached for earth energy, refined it to resonate with quartz, and probed the baby gargoyle as if I planned to work the quartz. The sensation was like trying to capture an echo. The gargoyle was quartz, but he was also so much more: He was alive. I twined fire around the earth magic and trickled wood, air, and water into the mix until I had the right magical resonance. I pressed the mixture into the hatchling. A backlash of pain and fear ricocheted through the magic—not from my actions, but from the horror the gargoyle had already endured. The gargoyle's feet and wings ended in acid-eaten, eroded lumps. Gasping for breath, I eased my magic out of the hatchling. My stomach heaved, but there was nothing to vomit.

When I glanced up, I met the healthy gargoyle's eyes,

seeing her anguish and anger. "I don't know what to do," I said, swiping at wet cheeks.

"You have to help him."

"I don't know how." Helplessly, I stared at the suffering gargoyle. His movements were weak. He was dying, drained of magic and in so much pain.

3

I wasn't lying: I had no idea what to do. But I couldn't do nothing.

I slid magic into the gargoyle, gritting my teeth against the avalanche of pain transmitted back to me. Closing my eyes, I sank into the quartz as I would into a normal project, feeling the pattern of the rock. The hatchling was vastly more complex than any quartz I'd touched before, containing thousands of intertwining striations hosting the intricate patterns of life. Quartz was a hardy mineral in all forms, yet this gargoyle felt like he would shatter in a gust of wind. Too much of his magic—his life—had been siphoned from him. More continued to leak from the raw wounds of his missing limbs. If I had any chance of saving the gargoyle's life, the wounds had to be sealed. Closing them wouldn't be good enough, though. Not if he was to have a future. His limbs needed to be regrown.

"I can't do this alone," I said, looking into the eyes of the stone panther. "I'm not strong enough." But maybe I would be if I used the magic leaking from the injured hatchling. I balked at the thought, then realized that even if I was okay with stealing the injured gargoyle's magic, I'd be depleting the very resource I was trying to replenish.

The panther hissed and snapped her tail in rhythmic pops. "Bring Herbert out here first," she finally said, keeping just outside the pentagram's circle.

I reached for the injured hatchling—Herbert—and he twitched, squealing, trying to escape me without any limbs or energy to use.

"Shh. It's okay. We're here to help." Herbert's rock body was too light, and my fear for the hatchling's fading life sent fresh tears dripping down my cheeks. Working quickly, I scuffed five of the chalk lines leading to the earth anchor; then I broke the outer circle.

The panther growled when I set Herbert down several paces from the abomination that had nearly killed him. She sniffed him, then me. I knelt and touched Herbert's toucan beak. His eyes were closed now, and I reached out with magic, fearing the worst.

"He's alive. Barely. We need to work fast."

"Sit," she ordered.

I sat, and the panther curled her bulk into my lap, claws flexed against my crossed calves.

A wellspring of gargoyle-enhanced magic dropped inside me. My stomach lurched at the free-fall sensation before I tapped into my magic and effortlessly pulled three times my usual amount. This is what it was like to be an FSPP.

With this level of power, I could do anything, even heal a gargoyle.

The hatchling was quartz. Even without enhancement, and despite being only a midlevel earth elemental, my quartz specialty was near FSPP level. With gargoyle enhancement, I could work quartz like a pentagram-linked earth elemental.

Using a delicate pulse of woven magic, I coaxed the jagged hatchling's side to grow.

The flame within Herbert flickered, and the beast went limp. Frantic, I pumped more fire into him, then traces of the other elements, and waited until he stabilized. The baby didn't have enough body or life left to grow new appendages, even with my influx of magic.

I sat back, trying to be analytical rather than emotional. This was a common problem with quartz. There was only so much manipulation a piece could take without the infusion of additional quartz. I prayed the same would apply to the gargoyle and thanked the gods that I was rarely without seed crystals. I placed a pearl-shaped clear crystal on the gargoyle's still side where his wing should have been and dove back in.

Coaxing the seed to grow was as familiar and easy as breathing, but connecting the gargoyle's complex internal networks to the lifeless seed and matching the seed crystal's growth patterns to the gargoyle's required all my skill and concentration. Just when I got the hang of it, having stretched almost an inch out of the seed crystal, the connecting fibers from the gargoyle stagnated.

Puzzled, I squinted at the half-wing lump. Rose quartz ran through clear quartz like veins, ending in a jagged edge. However, where the fibers refused to grow was smooth like the gargoyle's body. I hadn't done that. The stone panther hadn't, either. Her magic was a passive boost to mine, providing no input. Somehow, even while unconscious, Herbert was guiding the design, defining the shape of his wing as I regrew it. In awe, I refocused on the weave of magic. As I guessed, once I switched growth directions to flow toward the jagged edges, the hatchling's body responded to my manipulations again. Now that I knew what to feel for, I worked faster and finished the wing in minutes.

One healed appendage out of six made a meager impact on the gargoyle's suffering. Working diligently, I used seed crystals to grow stubby legs that ended in oversize paws. Then, easing the gargoyle over, I regrew the other wing. With each healed limb, the gargoyle's pain receded and the life seeping from him ebbed until he was whole—weak, but no longer dying.

A hollowness opened within me when the panther cut off her magic amplification. I released my magic and swayed against the backwash of exhaustion. The panther pushed from my lap to nuzzle the unconscious gargoyle. I watched the two hatchlings, realizing from their magical patterns that they were siblings, despite their radically different appearances.

A concussive boom rocked the ground, passing through me with a physical pulse. To the east, a giant fireball erupted against the pale horizon. Screams echoed through the block, too close for comfort. Lightning cut the night sky, followed by the shudder of an earthquake. Magic crackled in the air. Whoever the Fire Eaters had been after, they'd found them.

"We need to get out of here," I said.

The tiny stone panther's eyes glowed with fear. She seemed torn between fleeing and staying crouched over her brother.

"Come with me. I'll keep you both safe." Anywhere was safer than staying here. Getting outside the blight and back to Ms. Zuberrie's sounded like a good start. After that, we could work on a long-term plan.

Rapid-fire concussions rattled the loading dock, collapsing another section of roof in an earsplitting crash. Dust billowed over us. The sour copper taste of rust caught in my throat. I coughed and staggered to my feet after two trembling attempts. Healing Herbert had strained the bounds of my energy levels, physically and magically. But even if I'd been at full strength, I wouldn't have stuck around in warring gang territory.

The panther watched me, still looking undecided.

"Do you know the way back to my home?"

Finally, she nodded. I released a pent-up breath. I lifted Herbert, now asleep and healing, to my chest. It was like cradling a small boulder. My arms trembled.

The stone panther loped toward the dock's northern exit. Rubbing grit out of my eyes, I stumbled after her.

I tried to remain alert to my surroundings, but exhaustion deteriorated my focus. Keeping the panther in sight and staying on my feet were the best I could muster. Herbert gained weight with each step. After a few blocks, the sound of fighting faded and I paused long enough to stuff the hatchling under my shirt, tucking the cloth back in and cradling my arm under the cotton-covered bulk. With my shirt distributing the hatchling's weight, he felt a little lighter, and with Herbert hidden from view, I felt a little safer.

I wasn't the only person concerned with safety: Costly whole-house wards shimmered over most homes, and the number of blatant traps had doubled in the last half hour. The turf battle rocking the blight had everyone cowering in their safety zones.

Twice I heard city guards, once on flying platforms and once marching double time on foot. Both times, the panther took us through side alleys so our paths didn't cross. I had enough wherewithal to be thankful we were avoiding questioning, but mainly I lamented the extra steps the detours demanded of my drained body.

An eon later, the panther stopped, and I stared numbly at Ms. Zuberrie's house. The hatchling flapped up to my studio balcony, her flight path erratic and heavy. For the first time, it occurred to me that healing Herbert had drained her, too.

Grabbing the banister railing for support, I pulled myself up the stairs. I set Herbert at the foot of my bed, then fell face-first onto my comforter and into blackness.

4

"**W**ake up, girl. There's a baby gargoyle on the balcony," Kylie whispered against my ear. I jolted awake. Sunlight streamed through the bay windows, sparkling on the half dozen finished tubes on my worktable. Only six, when there needed to be twelve as of . . . a few hours from now. Impossible. I groaned and sat up. My head pounded. I rolled my shoulders to work out my neck's kink. Maybe if I got right to work, I could finish most of them before—

"Crap! Work!" I lurched from the bed. I was hours late. Without an explanation or notification. Silvia Jones had a zero-tolerance policy for tardiness. This was the only excuse she'd need to fire me. Unfortunately, I needed my job awhile longer while I built up my clientele. My gaze fell on the unfinished project again. If I didn't finish the vials, I wasn't going to have a business. I needed the referrals this project would bring.

"Did you hear me, Mika?" Kylie asked. She plopped onto the bed, her blue eyes tracking my frantic movements.

"Yes. Gargoyle. She's still here." I scribbled a note:

Battling deadly illness; refusing to go into the light. Maybe Silvia would take pity on me.

"She? You know about the gargoyle? What are you writing? Wait—you expect Ms. Be-Sick-on-Your-Own-Time Jones to believe that? Let me do it." Kylie formed a bubble of air magic and recited a compelling plea on my behalf, wrapped it in tight bands of air, and sent it rocketing off to Silvia's message box. I stared enviously after it. Kylie was a strong air elemental—almost an FSPP. I wouldn't have been able to create a message bubble that large, and it would have traveled no faster than walking speed once released. "Did you like my emphasis on how contagious you are?" Kylie grinned. "Now, spill. What's with the gargoyle?"

Recounting the previous night's adventure made it feel surreal. While I spoke, I watched the panther hatchling, who was perched on the balcony railing, tight against the house and all but hidden in the eave's shadow. She sat still as stone, unblinking, unbreathing. Unnerving. Kylie's mouth was hanging open by the time I finished.

"Wow, Mika. That was . . ." Her blue eyes grew round. "Do you think the abused hatchling was connected to the Fire Eater attack last night? The *Chronicle* said they took out four blocks. The casualties are in the double digits. FSPP investigators are involved."

"I know it was," I said. "Where's Herbert? Did you see him outside?"

Kylie shook her head. I could see her mind working over everything I'd told her. When I noticed the lump under the covers at her hip, I grinned. Flipping back the covers, I revealed the sleeping form of Herbert. Kylie leapt to her feet.

"Oh my goodness! I almost sat on him."

Herbert's long stone toucan beak stretched wide in a yawn

and his eyes blinked open. When he saw us, he shrieked and leapt into the air. Heavy rose-veined crystal wings buffeted us, and we dove for cover in opposite directions.

"Open the door!" I yelled.

Kylie lurched for the balcony door and threw it open. The winged panther woke and spun. One moment she was a statue, the next she was sailing into the room. The panther caught Herbert in her paws and dropped him to the ground, pinning him in place. Kylie and I watched, wide-eyed, as the baby gargoyles snarled at each other. It took several minutes for the panther to calm Herbert, and when she finally let him up, Kylie and I both took a step back.

"She's okay," the panther said, pointing at me with a wing. "She saved you."

Seeing Herbert calm down, I eased to the floor and Kylie mirrored me. "I'm Mika. This is my best friend, Kylie. She's okay, too."

Kylie nodded enthusiastically. "I want to help, if you need it."

The panther shook her head. "Herbert and I are the last of our nest."

"No, Anya. They live." Herbert's voice was higher pitched than his sister's.

"I only sense you," Anya said. She lifted her cat face, scenting the air.

"They're shielded by the bad man. The one who took us."

My heart sank.

With Kylie doing most of the questioning, we learned that Herbert was one of four hatchlings taken from their wilderness nest and caged. Only Anya, who had been away from the nest when it was ambushed, had been spared.

"He sold me. For money!" Herbert said. "Humans are evil."

"Not all of them. Mika healed you. I helped."

I thought Anya sounded proud, and I couldn't tell if it was of herself or me.

"Why did you choose Mika last night for help? Why not a full-spectrum elemental?" Kylie asked.

It was a reasonable question, and I tried not to be offended. I also recognized that tone. Kylie had gone into reporter mode. She may work at the local coffee shop, but Kylie's ambition was to be a famous journalist, and she was well versed in the requisite story-sniffing rudeness.

"I don't know what a full spectrum is," Anya said. She sat on her haunches, and her wings rustled. In a normal cat, I would have said she was embarrassed. "I thought Mika was a gargoyle."

"You what?" I asked.

"The magic you were doing. It smelled like a gargoyle. If I'd known you were human . . . I don't like humans. I don't trust them."

With good reason. From what I could tell, Anya and Herbert were only a few weeks old, and their only interactions with humans, other than with me and Kylie, had been horrific.

"Where are the others?" Kylie asked.

"In cages." Herbert's long tail lashed back and forth, bunching the area rug beneath him. "The bad man is going to sell them like he did me." The hatchling's tail stilled and he trembled in place. Anya leaned into him, and a gravelly purr rumbled in her throat.

"A black market," Kylie breathed. Her bright blue eyes lit up, and I didn't need telepathy to know she was seeing her byline beneath the front-page headline. "You can count on us to rescue your siblings," she announced.

"We can tell the authorities. They'll know where to look."

"We can do more than that." Forming complex bubbles of air magic, Kylie spoke into them, whispering, "Gargoyle hatchlings, gargoyles for sale," and a dozen other phrases, one per bubble. When she finished, each collapsed into a boomerang shape and whirled out into the city, fading from sight almost immediately. Even for Kylie, the rumor scouts formed and moved fast. She gave me wide eyes, and I examined the hatchlings. In his fear, Herbert had leaked a thin current of magic, and Kylie's rumor scouts had soaked it up.

"As soon as those return, we'll know where they're kept," Kylie said, recovering from her surprise.

Information would be good, but I wasn't going to delay notifying the people who actually knew what to do if they encountered a black magic wielder. So as Kylie got ready for work, I rushed to the nearest guard office.

Hours later, I dragged myself back to Ms. Zuberrie's. The excursion had been a waste of time and energy. The guards took one look at me and my midlevel elemental skills and dismissed my recounting of healing Herbert as attention-seeking lies, especially when I told them I'd been in the blight just blocks away from the huge Fire Eater battle. I hadn't thought to bring the only two individuals who could substantiate my story—Herbert and Anya.

Despite their refusal to offer assistance, the guards had insisted on following protocol, which required filing a report about my "wild and foolish" claims. After making me wait over an hour, they passed me off to a trainee hardly old enough to be assigned a desk. He spent forty-five minutes trying to trick me into confessing to taking hallucinogens before ushering me to the door with a final, "We'll keep your report on file." It had sounded like a threat, as if the guards were now monitoring my sanity.

"Stupid bigoted guards." I stomped up the porch stairs. I was no closer to finding the kidnapped hatchlings *and* I'd lost precious work hours. I opened the front door to Ms. Zuberrie's and came face-to-face with my deadline in the form of a stout dark-haired woman with an upturned nose and sour expression: Althea Stoneward, healer apprentice for the prestigious Blackwell-Zakrzewska Clinic and my contact for the unfinished project upstairs. My stomach sank even as I plastered on a smile.

5

"I have been waiting," Althea announced.

"I'm so sorry. I need a little more time—"

"More time? We have been more than generous with our deadline. Are you breaking your contract?"

"No! Of course not." I eased into the foyer, shut the front door, and cast a furtive glance into the living room and then the dining room, relieved to see we were alone. "I have six finished and—"

"The order was for twelve."

"I ran into . . . time constraints." After my experience at the guard station, I was reluctant to attempt the truth with Althea. If she thought I was claiming to be an FSPP gargoyle healer, she would cancel my contract and see my reputation ruined beyond repair. "Let me get you the six I finished."

Before she could protest, I darted upstairs. When I returned with the six vials wrapped in cloth, her round face was red with irritation and her arms were crossed. I grabbed a vial and thrust it into her hands. She glared, then turned her attention to the quartz. Lifting it to the light, she examined it in silence, looking for flaws I knew she wouldn't find. Wordlessly, she scrutinized the rest.

"I need just one more day," I said, fingers crossed behind my back.

She rewrapped the vials and scowled down her upturned nose at me. "One day, Mika Stillwater. You'll deduct twenty percent from your fee for the delay, too." She slammed the door behind her.

I collapsed against the nearby wall, thanking the gods for small favors. Then I trudged up the stairs to get to work on my new impossible deadline. There was still a chance I could salvage my dreams. Twenty percent loss of pay would leave me with enough money for a down payment on the Pinnacle Pentagon shop and apartment—I'd just have to keep my day job a little longer to make ends meet. *A temporary setback,* I promised my heavy heart.

After taking a quick shower and inhaling a handful of blueberries, I settled at my desk and selected a seed crystal from my stash. On second thought, I dropped a handful of seed crystals into my pockets, just in case. *In case an injured gargoyle waltzes by?*

I squelched a wave of guilt. I'd done what I could to help find Anya and Herbert's siblings. I was a midlevel earth elemental, not an FSPP air elemental. Aside from alerting the guards, I had no other way of locating stolen property of any kind, let alone kidnapped magical creatures. I could only hope that Kylie's rumor scouts produced information that would make the guards believe me. I'd be sure to take Anya and Herbert along then, too. In the meantime, fretting wasn't going to produce any leads, and at least this way I wasn't neglecting my responsibilities.

I cleared my thoughts to focus on the crystal in front of me. Pulling strands of elemental earth energy and fine-tuning it to resonate with quartz, I fed it to the seed crystal. With astonishing ease, the seed grew and reshaped.

A faint hum cocooned my magic. Far from annoying, it soothed my restlessness and resonated with my magic, amplifying it. I recognized it as gargoyle influence, but I was surprised when I could follow the sensation to the source, locating Anya by only the feel of her magic. For reasons I wasn't going to question, Anya was generously boosting my magic from where she huddled in the shadows on the balcony railing with Herbert.

The vial shattered. In my distraction, I had stretched the crystal too thin. Grimacing, I pulled my thoughts back to my work. Gargoyle enhancement was helpful only if I focused.

The next vial broke when Kylie burst into my room, startling me into dropping it. I gritted my teeth and used a quick sweep of air to pull the shards into a pile before turning to my friend. Kylie was already talking.

"It's tonight! I've got the location and the time and everything. I can't believe it. Those rumor scouts returned so complete! Normally I get a snippet or a line or two, but these were whole conversations. I bet you I'd recognize the voices of the people if I heard them again."

"Whoa. Slow down. What's tonight?" I asked.

"The hatchling auction. I know how to get in, too, but we've got to hurry."

My stomach clenched with dread. "We? Don't you mean the guards?"

"So they believed you?"

"No."

"Okay." Kylie didn't pause, and I realized she'd never expected the guards to believe my incredulous rescue tale. "They're doing a demonstration first. That's what the auction guy, Walter, said. I mean, I think he's the auctioneer.

He gave the first order; the rest just repeated it to the others. He said he'd provide a demonstration first . . . to showcase the hatchlings' usefulness." I could see Kylie absorb the horror of her words, and her excitement deflated.

"When?"

She glanced out the windows at the evening light. "At dusk."

"Where?"

"New Hope, in the south temple."

Of course. On the west side of Lincoln River, the suburb of New Hope was isolated from the city of Terra Haven and preferred it that way. New Hope was what the blight wanted to be when it grew up, populated with profitable, if questionable, establishments. The dilapidated south temple was the perfect cover for a clandestine black market.

"They have all three of the hatchlings," Kylie said. "If we don't rescue them before they're sold, they're all going to die."

"We can't just mosey in and demand they hand over the hatchlings."

"That's exactly what we'll do. Well, not *exactly*. We'll buy our way in. It's an auction, after all. The door fee is only ten thousand—"

"*Only ten thousand!* Where would we get that much money?"

"You've got some savings, right?"

A little over six thousand, and that was slated for the lease on my ideal showroom at the Pinnacle Pentagon Center. I'd been saving for three years, sacrificing and scrimping to make my dream of independence a reality. Endless nights, I had worked on painstaking projects like these vials to build a reputation in an oversaturated market, and people were starting to take notice. I was on the precipice of success, but it all depended on opening my shop and going into business for myself full-time. If I was forced to keep my day job to make ends meet, I was going to lose this hard-won momentum, and potential clients would look elsewhere for their needs.

Anya dropped to the wooden deck with a thud and prowled into my studio. "Did you find them?" she asked.

"Yes, but they're still being held by the bad man," Kylie said.

Woken by Anya's movement, Herbert followed on heavy wings, his flight path as haphazard as a falling leaf.

I remembered the lump of rock I'd mistaken him for last night and his wails of pain. Someone had sold him to people who burned him, devoured his life for their magical gain, and left him to die a slow, painful death. That same monster was planning to do it again to three more hatchlings.

It shamed me to realize it was taking serious consideration to decide between delaying my dreams and saving the hatchlings' lives. The decision should have been immediate and required no thought.

"I've only got a little over six thousand," I said.

"I've got some, too." Kylie darted toward the door.

"Wait. Can we both get in for ten thousand?"

Kylie slowed and turned back to me. "No. Only one of us."

"It should be me," I was flabbergasted to hear myself say. Kylie only nodded. "But then what? It's not like we can buy the hatchlings and I don't have the power to take them by force. I can't stop . . . I'm not trained . . . I'm . . ." *I'm only a midlevel earth elemental,* I finished silently.

"You have to stall the auction. Get us more time." Kylie

turned to address Anya. "You and your brother can help me. If you talked with the guards—"

"Guards! No! I won't go back." Herbert curled into a tight ball, rose quartz–veined crystal wings wrapping around his quivering body.

6

"**B**ack?" I echoed.

"To him," Herbert said.

I shared a look with Kylie. "You were taken by a Terra Haven guard?"

"How do you know?" Kylie asked gently.

"Because he said so." Herbert's answer was muffled and garbled by the chattering of his jaw.

"Anyone could say—"

"Was he in uniform? Did his shirt have any symbols?" I asked, interrupting Kylie.

Herbert's head jerked in a nod. "A circle with a zigzag line, a leaf, a drop, some squiggles, and a flame."

Having spent the day staring at this exact logo on the shirts of the guards at the station, I recognized Herbert's description of the icons for the constructive cycle that formed the Terra Haven guard badge. Kylie and I shared a look.

"This bad Walter guy isn't a guard, no matter what he wore," Kylie said. "Guards protect."

"I swear, the guards will help us," I said.

"*You* can save them," Anya said, her pleading gaze fixed on me. "You saved Herbert. You can save the others."

Kylie glanced at the clock on the wall. "We've got to try, Mika. You delay them. I'll bring the *good* guys. Now that we have the auction location, they can't ignore us."

If we believed that, I wouldn't be going to the auction at all.

Kylie must have read my doubts. "You just have to get us a little time."

"You really believe you can convince them?"

"I won't let you down, Mika." Kylie dashed to her room to fetch her money.

I watched Herbert shiver in his traumatized huddle. Anya stared at me with a faith I didn't deserve.

I grabbed my life savings, hesitating with the weight of the money in my hands before stuffing it into a nondescript satchel, feeling like I was plunging my hopes and dreams into the dark enclosure with it.

I TOOK A PUBLIC AIR BUS ACROSS TOWN, PACING IN THE AISLE the whole way. There were faster modes of travel—flying platforms, personal air taxis, gryphons—but none within my skill or price range. The sun had dipped behind the ragged skyline by the time I disembarked, and while my instincts insisted I approach the temple cautiously, time was running out. I forced myself to sprint through the darkening streets.

The last time I'd visited the south temple, I was five. In sixteen years, even the temple's illusions of its former glory had deteriorated. Exterior walls were cracked, and in several places, giant gaps exposed the interior to the elements. The scrap of park remaining around the temple was musty with decay. Hardy vines strangled eroding statues and sucked the life from the withered trees looming over the entrance. Not a single lamp was lit.

Dead leaves crackled underfoot as I raced across the grounds to the entrance, praying this foolish stunt wouldn't get me killed. This wasn't going to be like last night. I wasn't rushing in after the fact. I would be in the midst of black magic wielders, rubbing elbows with powerful criminals and trying to thwart a corrupt guard.

I'd wracked my brain for an alternate plan the entire bus ride and drawn a blank. All my hopes rested on Kylie being more convincing with the guards than I had been.

Copper chains rattled in the shadowy depths of the vestibule. It was a distinctive sound, one that, once heard, was never forgotten. Kludde. I froze, ice running through my veins. My heart hammered against my rib cage as it approached. Fleeing would do no good. A kludde could match me at any speed. I gathered fire in my thoughts, ready to throw pure magic at the beast if it charged. If I was lucky, setting its face on fire might slow it a little.

I saw the copper chain links first, each as thick as my wrist. Then the kludde's eyes, over a foot higher than mine, caught a glimmer of fading light. I shrank back, careful to not move my feet, trying not to behave like prey even as my gibbering instincts insisted I was. Looking part Great Dane, part wolf, and part madness, the kludde towered over me, standing on its hind legs. Its coarse coat consisted of layers of the darkest shadows. Sinister yellow eyes pierced me, intelligent and malevolent. Enormous crow's wings rustled against its backside. My throat constricted, cutting off air.

Please don't let it open its wings. Open wings meant it was hunting, and I was the only victim in sight.

The heavy chain snapped, and the kludde growled, tossing a glare over its shoulder. Behind the beast loomed a person, though in the darkness I couldn't be sure he was human. He was tall enough to be a troll, with expansive shoulders to match. His face looked human. His dark eyes terrified me more than the kludde's.

"It's a f-fi-fine night for a p-picnic," I stammered, repeating the code words from Kylie's rumor scouts.

"It would be better under a full moon." The man's voice was a pitch above a growl. Drool dripped from the kludde's open mouth as it tracked me.

"The darkness suits my mood," I said. These lines had sounded more ridiculous in Kylie's bright apartment.

The kludde snarled, hackles raised, when the man yanked it back, leaving space for me to squeeze inside the maw of the temple. I stepped forward on trembling legs, only to be stopped by a beefy arm thrown across my path.

"Money," he growled.

The kludde's hot breath parted my hair. I was pinned between the man and kludde, trapped. Either of them could kill me before I could so much as scream. I jammed a hand into my satchel and pulled the money out. The man snorted at the fluttering bills before snatching them from my shaking hand and counting them. I waited for his grunt of assent, then fled into the temple's dark confines.

There was just enough light to avoid the majority of rubble, and I didn't slow until I escaped the kludde's sight. A few twists beyond the main entrance, I heard muffled voices and remembered my purpose. Another turn, and the floor dropped away to shadowy basement stairs. I hesitated on the landing, heartbeat thundering in my ears. I could still

turn back. No one but the door guard—and the kludde—
had seen me. I could leave safely.

*And have lost your savings on top of abandoning three hatch-
lings to be tortured and killed.* I clutched the seed crystals in
my pocket and forced my feet down the stairs.

7

I didn't know what to expect, but it wasn't the brightly lit chamber I found. At one time, the room had functioned as a place for private ceremonies, with an enormous pentagram etched into the floor, circled by a groove of colored stones to represent each element. The room could hold at least fifty comfortably. It felt cavernous with only five people in it.

Everyone turned to stare at me, and I paused on the threshold. A man and woman wore matching masks that concealed the top half of their faces, and the perpetually shifting layers of the woman's dress disguised her body even better. For that movement, an air spell worth twice tonight's door fee had to be woven into the fabric. A third person wore a simple cloth hood that covered all but his eyes, but his abnormal height—easily equal to that of the kludde— and wide shoulders marked him as male. Beside him stood a man in a university professor's uniform of tweed and corduroy. However, a faint shimmer at the periphery of his face revealed a poorly connected seam in his illusion spell;

the benevolent grandfather's face was a fake. Standing apart from the main group was a dark-haired tattooed man who would have looked at home in the blight. *Mercenary,* I thought. Though no weapons were visible on him, I was sure that he could have given the guard upstairs a good fight. He wore no camouflage, illusion or otherwise.

I hadn't considered a disguise, and now I cursed my lack of foresight. In jeans, a pale blue T-shirt, and my black canvas button-up jacket, with a student's leather satchel draped diagonally across my chest, I looked as out of place as I felt. I slipped into the room and skirted to the left.

I fidgeted while we waited, staying well clear of the room's other occupants. With no distractions, my doubts overwhelmed all other thoughts. What if I couldn't stall the auction? What if Walter didn't bring the hatchlings here? Even if Kylie convinced the guards to arrest everyone, we might never find them.

No, we'd find at least one. The demonstration hatchling. The thought wasn't reassuring.

In a few minutes, a dozen new people filtered into the room, restricting my movement. Most, again, were disguised, and the few who weren't radiated strong I'd-like-to-kill-you vibes. Still, I received the most curious stares. Everyone could see I didn't belong there.

"Welcome." The disembodied male voice turned everyone's head. A seamless illusion dropped, opening the round room over three feet in every direction. I wasn't the only one to gasp at the power display.

Walter stepped forward from where he'd been observing us behind the illusion. There was nothing about the man's appearance that identified him as evil incarnate. He was slight, barely taller than my five-nine, with sandy brown hair and green eyes. He had a boyish smile. If I'd seen him in a café, I might have found him handsome; with a wounded gargoyle in his grip, however, he was repulsive.

The mutilated hatchling was hardly larger than my cupped hands, half the size of Anya. He trembled in a magic trap in Walter's hand, his variegated citrine body glistening in the bright spell lights attached to the ceiling. The tips of his feet and wings had been burned away, and they twitched spasmodically. His little, expressive lion face—complete with mobile eyebrows never found on a real lion—was pinched with pain. Enormous golden eyes scanned the room, glossy and unfocused. Every so often, he lifted his head, mouth stretched open, but no sound made it past the muzzle of air woven to dampen his cries.

Rage flooded my body until I shook with it instead of fear.

"Tonight you have the unprecedented opportunity to elevate yourself to a full spectrum, with limitless power and limitless possibilities." Walter's voice carried through the still room. "There is untapped potential in each gargoyle, even one so small as this." He hoisted the mutilated hatchling into the air. I looked away from his pitiful, soundless cries in time to see the double doors to the exit swing soundlessly closed and an illusion cover it. I rubbed my sweaty palms on my pants and willed a platoon of guards to burst through the illusion.

"The power is there for the taking—for the right price." Walter's smile turned hard. "But first, a small demonstration for the skeptics."

Walter stepped into the center of the pentagram, hatchling in hand, and everyone crowded to the walls, several people running to clear the pentagram's closure circle.

Walter's eyes slid closed, and he breathed deep. On a long exhale, his eyes opened to half-mast and a small, self-satisfied smile curled his lips. A wall of raw magic raced through the star's lines, then rushed to fill the circle containing the pentagram. The magic pulled from the baby gargoyle's wounded limbs, and a fine dust drifted toward Walter's feet as the magic ate away the hatchling's stone flesh.

Around the room, people gasped and murmured at the display of power most hadn't seen outside of a full temple ceremony hosted by five linked FSPPs. The vultures surged forward, jostling one another until they ringed Walter and the pentagram. I held back, sickened by the sight of the magic leeching from the struggling hatchling.

"Some of you might have heard of my first customer and the tiny explosion they unleashed on the blight last night." Walter winked. The Fire Eaters' battle had been splashed across every news feed today. No one could have missed it. "What would you do with that amount of power?"

From across the room, I felt his magic build as he wove together the five elements. A sphere popped into existence around him, hesitated, then expanded in all directions at once. There wasn't time to flee, and there was nowhere to go. The wall of magic slammed into the crowd, and the bidders swayed like a human ripple in a pond. Then it squeezed over me, a solid slimy sheet of magic stretching against my skin as if I were naked. I fought to stay on my feet. My magic swelled, uncalled and ineffectual. Then Walter's bubble snapped together behind me and raced outward, leaving a greasy film behind. I staggered forward, but my senses tracked the magic out and up, where it mushroomed to encase the entire temple. A ward. A monstrously powerful ward. One that would keep out anyone attempting to pass. One at least seven times larger than a single FSPP could create. I pictured a wall of guards pitting themselves ineffectually against the ward. A chill of fear made me shiver.

The excitement in the room ratcheted higher. I caught a glimpse of the hatchling and wanted to cry. His head lolled limp, but I knew he wasn't dead. Magic still leeched from his open wounds, feeding directly to Walter.

Hang in there, little guy.

Someone slid behind me, and I spun to see what they were doing, trusting no one in this room at my back. It was the professor. He wasn't paying any attention to me or to Walter's performance at the center of the pentagram. He was examining the walls. I watched him pause in front of a section of plaster and squint. He leaned back and forth, then touched the wall, pulling back with a jerk.

I hadn't realized I'd stepped closer to him until he reached inside his professor's coat and pulled out a long, slender knife. I backpedaled, far too slow. He seized my bicep, and the steel point of the knife pricked my neck.

"Don't be scared, girl." His hot breath whispered against my ear, and I shuddered.

"What—"

"Shh."

A few people near us noticed the professor's knife against my throat and sidled away. There'd be no help from these lowlifes.

"Reach out and touch the wall. Right there. Let's see what happens."

Walter's voice droned in the background, but his words didn't make sense in my acute panic. I could feel the swell of his magic. In my mind, I saw the gargoyle's limbs crumble away with the surge of magic siphoned from him.

The knife jabbed my neck and I hissed at the sting.

Where was Kylie? How had this ever seemed like a good plan? If it hadn't been obvious that I was way out of my element before, it was painfully clear now. I had no fighting skills, no defense training. I'd never had to think about it before. And right now, all I could think was that I didn't want to die.

"Now, girl!" the professor hissed. The stench of sweat and garlic oozed from him, coiling in my throat.

I stretched my fingers toward the wall. The faint tell-tale glimmer of yet another illusion masked this section of the wall. Just how strong was Walter? And how much longer could the hatchling survive?

Move away. Look away. Don't touch. I pulled my hand back.

"Push through it," the professor said, emphasizing his words with the pressure of his knife.

I reached forward again, and again I felt a compulsion to retreat. An illusion combined with a subtle ward, one designed for people to not even notice it was there.

I gritted my teeth and shoved my fingertips into the ward. Flames licked my flesh. With a yelp, I jerked free and examined my skin. My fingertips were red, pulsing with the pain of a burn.

"Hurts, don't it? Let's see what happens if you get closer." The professor shoved me with a strength that belied his guise of age.

"No!" I fell against the warded illusion and my cry strangled on a scream of agony. The ward ensnared me. Fire engulfed my body. I convulsed, every twist and flail winding me tighter in the trap, ratcheting the pain. I screamed again as my skin melted. I scrabbled for water magic and doused the ward, and the ward soaked it up. I couldn't break free!

I wrenched my head back toward the professor. A sea of faces watched me writhe, not a single one looking concerned. *Help me!* I begged, but I couldn't form the words between screams.

8

My vision blackened, and I lashed out with magic again, desperate. Without control, my raw magic reverted to the strongest, most familiar form: quartz earth energy. I stabbed at the ward, and it split, a tiny fracture tearing like wet cloth under my weight. I fell. I couldn't find my hands to brace myself, and I slammed into the rock floor behind the ward.

Residual panic launched me to my knees, then kept me conscious when the pain washed over me. My entire body felt raw from skin down to bone.

"There's one in every crowd," Walter said, tsking. "If anyone else would like to test me, you're welcome to die, too. Now, bidding starts at fifty thousand."

Walter's words registered. That had been a death spell, not just a ward! I jerked toward the ceremony room. It was like looking through murky water. No one looked my way, not even the professor. Somehow I had survived, and Walter couldn't tell that his murderous ward had failed.

Now would be a really good time to show up, Kylie. There was no way I was making it back through that ward. I was trapped until the auction was over and Walter's spells dropped. If he found me alive after that, I had no delusion I'd remain breathing for long. Stuck on this side of the ward, it would be impossible to delay the auction, too.

I dropped my head to rest on the floor, taking shallow breaths until the pain receded enough to think. I wasn't going to wait here to be discovered.

My eyes slowly adjusted to the gloomy light coming through the wall illusion, and I examined the small, dark alcove. I was in a storage room of some sort. The walls were smooth and wrapped back around the circular ceremonial room where the auction was currently under way. I felt along the wall, taking baby steps deeper into the darkness, until my foot crunched into something hard.

I reached blindly for the object. It gave with a tingle beneath my tender fingertips, like a cloth of magic. A ward. I jerked back. I'd had more than enough of Walter's wards.

I glanced back toward the death ward. It was out of sight around the bend. I could either blunder along into another ward that might kill me, or I could chance creating a little light.

Drawing a trickle of fire magic, I set a small pea-size flame in the air in front of me.

Two tiny sets of terror-filled baby gargoyle eyes glowed in the faint light. I dropped to my knees in front of them, feeling hope for the first time.

The hatchlings' mouths moved in panicked cries caught behind soundproofed traps, and they struggled futilely against magical bonds.

"It's okay. I'm here to help. Anya sent me," I whispered. They quivered and swiveled heads on weak necks, looking for an escape that didn't exist.

When I reached toward the first one, he keened wildly,

thrashing as much as the bonds permitted. He looked like a baby Chinese dragon, with a wide, square head and feathery rock tufts behind his ears. The net around him glowed red, the magic matching his blood-orange carnelian body getting brighter the more he struggled. His right side was perfect and whole. His left, though . . . Magic sucked into the net from the ragged wounds on the bottom of his two left feet and the tip of his left wing. Even without the trap holding him, there was no way the injured baby dragon could escape.

Cautious of both Walter's magic and the hatchling, I hovered my hand above the trap. The energy pattern was almost familiar—weaves of earth and fire with swirls of wind and a whirlpool of water. The earth energy resonated with quartz, a pattern I was intimately tuned to. Seed crystals fused to the floor acted as focal knots for the chains of magic as well as anchors, holding the net—and the hatchling—in place. A subtle band of magic stretched from the net to the death ward around the corner, sustaining it. Since Walter had created the ward, any excess magic drained from the hatchling would feed into him. It was a brilliant design —from Walter's perspective.

I had no idea how to proceed. I had no experience with negating black magic traps. However, I couldn't predict how much longer the auction would last or how long it would take Kylie to convince the guards. I had to improvise, and freeing the hatchlings was a good start. I wasn't going to get a better opportunity. Gathering my resolve, I grabbed a seed crystal anchor.

It wouldn't budge, no matter how much I strained. I couldn't force a finger through a hole in the net, either. A clean slice of solid, five-elements magic only made the hatchling spasm in pain. Balancing my elemental magic to match Walter's and feeding it into the crystal made the trap hum and the hatchling convulse. I jerked back and swiped sweat from my forehead. Working *with* the net wasn't the answer. I needed to counter it.

Fire burns wood, wood breaks up earth, earth stops air, air dries water, water extinguishes fire. It was the destructive element cycle every child learned by the time they could talk, and I chanted it now to focus my thoughts.

With surgical precision honed from long hours of delicate work, I sliced the earth magic channeled through the quartz with an equal level of wood magic. Earth collapsed and fire burned bright, feeding off the new wood energy. The hatchling tried to bite me, but he hit the bonds of magic and flopped back, exhausted.

"I'm sorry, little guy," I whispered. I added a trace of fire to expunge all wood, then doused the trap with water, pouring my magic over the fire faster and faster until it was extinguished. The net morphed in a blink, spinning the deluge of water magic into whirlpool patterns. The gargoyle's magic sucked from his wounds in a gush and he passed out.

Panicked, I threw air into the net, drying the water with a concentrated blast. It took more effort than extinguishing the fire, my elemental contributions strengthening the net even as I fought it. I was panting by the time the last drop of water magic evaporated. Only air whipped through the net now, but it dried up the hatchling's life with maniacal vigor. Grabbing earth magic, I dammed the air at each seed crystal. The first three were the hardest, the air pummeling the blockades of earth, disrupting my concentration as I created the next, but by the time I'd dammed five of the seven seed crystals, the air energy had fizzled down to a gentle breeze. I plugged the last two crystals, and the net dissipated. Magic leeched from the unconscious hatchling, but it was no longer actively siphoned.

I lifted my shirt hem with a trembling hand and wiped the sweat from my face. One down, one to go. I crawled toward the other gargoyle, this one a mutilated cygnet, though it took a long stare to make sense of the bulbous body and slender neck. With only one identifying wing tight against her body, the hatchling was a gross mimicry of a Thanksgiving dinner platter. Her rock feathers were a spectrum of purple, pink, and orange agate, as was the cage sucking away her life. Her body was almost the size of my head, making her the largest of all the hatchlings. She snaked her beak at me, eyes wild with pain.

I already felt like I'd worked a full shift at Jones and Sons, drained physically and magically from destroying the first net. But I'd succeeded in weakening Walter at least a little. I was congratulating myself as I rested until I realized that without the dragon hatchling's extra power feeding Walter through the ward, Walter was pulling more magic from the remaining two hatchlings.

The thought made me pause. If I removed the net from the cygnet, all the drain would be on the hatchling Walter held for demonstration. The lion had already looked close to death. Would my rescue of these hatchlings kill him?

Did I have a choice? Once Walter finished the bidding, he would collect these hatchlings. If I didn't act now, my hesitation would take away the one advantage I had: surprise.

Grimly, I bent to work on the cygnet's net. I knew what to expect this time, and while I countered the surges of each element faster, it was no less draining on my energy reserves. At least when I finished, the cygnet was still cognizant.

I collapsed against the wall. Urgency warred with weariness. The light illuminating the bend of the wall was brighter. Without the reinforcing magic from the hatchlings' nets, the illusion and ward covering the entrance had weakened. Similarly, the sounds of the auction room were no longer muted. I could hear Walter's voice and those of the bidders. The bidding had escalated to astronomical amounts, but it also sounded like it was winding down. So far, everyone was still focused on Walter at the center of the magic-filled pentagram, but I knew it wouldn't be long before someone noticed the flimsy illusion. Especially Walter. At my side, the cygnet was wisely silent.

"Triage time," I whispered. Plucking seed crystals from my pocket, I surged quartz-tuned earth element magic, equal parts fire and a balance of wood, air, and water through it and into the unconscious stone dragon, starting with his front foot, clamping my teeth against the agonizing backlash.

Just as with Herbert, the dragon guided the growth of the seed crystals, defining the shape of his limbs even as I wove and stretched the complicated amalgam of elements. I looked up after the dragon's front leg was whole to find the other hatchling watching with intent, glowing eyes.

"I told you, I'm here to help," I whispered. The world went fuzzy when I swung my head back to the dragon. Exhaustion was catching up with me fast, but there wasn't time to rest. I could only be grateful that the hatchlings weren't as injured as Herbert had been. Without Anya's assistance, regrowing the minor damage to the hatchling's limbs taxed my magical limits.

The dragon regained consciousness when I finished

growing his back leg. He leapt to his new red-veined crystal feet, threw his head back, and loosed a shriek. I grabbed his muzzle and clamped his jaw shut. The dragon yanked from my hold, whipping his head to stare at the cygnet, then down at his feet, then finally up at me.

Voices swelled, and I knew my luck had just run out.

9

I cast through my repertoire of skills for something resembling a weapon. There was nothing I could create that another slightly stronger elemental couldn't destroy. A string of candle flames—the largest fire I could build without something flammable to burn—wouldn't hold off a house cat, let alone the greedy masses and psychopathic black magic practitioners in the next room. Not even my stronger quartz skills would help me here. I couldn't form a quartz wall strong enough to stop someone. The only ward I knew how to create on a large scale was a tint to block the sun for mornings I wanted to sleep in.

Anything's better than nothing. I grabbed earth element, tinting it the deepest onyx of smoky quartz, so dark it was almost black, then formed a sheet of air and bound them together across the storage room opening, patching the illusion. If anyone looked into the nook, they'd see nothing but a dark shadow. The only problem with my solution—okay, *one* of the many problems with my solution—was it cut off my light, too. I fed a little fire into the pinprick of flame I had created earlier, stretching it to about an inch long, and placed it on the far side of the hatchlings.

In the flickering light, two pairs of glowing eyes watched me. The dragon shifted on his new crystal legs, whined softly, and rested his head on my knee as if in apology. I gave him a pat with hands numb with fear and got back to work. Fortunately, the dragon's wings were tiny, smaller than Herbert's despite the dragon being bigger, and it took only a few moments to regrow the mutilated appendage. The instant the hatchling was whole, a gush of energy surged into me, pushing exhaustion aside.

"Thank you," I whispered.

A shuffle of footsteps drew closer, audible over the growing murmurs in the crowd.

"You're flirting with death touching that ward," Walter barked.

"I can see through it, and I don't see the dead girl," a woman said from a few feet away. There was more shuffling and several curses and yelps of pain.

"Stand clear," Walter ordered, sounding like he was right behind me.

We were out of time. I threw open the top flap of my satchel and snatched the cygnet around the middle, stuffing her inside, head up, just in case gargoyles needed to breathe. I did my best not to touch her open wounds, but it was a tight fit in the bag, and the leather scraped the swan's sides. She whimpered but didn't protest. There was no space left for the dragon.

Grunting, I tugged thirty pounds of solid rock to the wall, then laid the flap across the cygnet's head, leaving it gapped at either end for air. I scooped the dragon up and showed him the space between the bag and the wall.

"Hide," I urged. Trusting eyes blinked once at me; then

the hatchling wriggled his sinuous body into the small gap, curling his stone tail tight to the leather satchel. I wove another tinting ward over the bag, pulling color from the plaster wall and stone floor into the ward. It was illusion on a scale normally unachievable for me, but with the dragon gargoyle's enhancement, it was almost easy.

A backlash of magic slapped my body, and the oily pressure of Walter's gigantic ward disappeared with the sting. Exclamations echoed through the nook.

"I thought you said nothing could get through that ward," someone accused.

I rubbed my arms. Did that mean the lion hatchling was dead?

"Wait—" Walter cried.

The room erupted in noise. In rapid succession, I heard the unmistakable sounds of flesh hitting flesh, the ring of steel being drawn, and then the deafening crack of thrown lightning. Screams pierced the ringing in my ears.

Should I grab the hatchlings and make a run for it? No. Rushing through a crowd of panicked felons with the hatchlings they coveted was suicidal. Plus, I had no idea where the little lion was. Or even if he still lived.

Against every instinct, I remained crouched in the storage room.

"Halt! Terra Haven guards! Show me your hands!"

The authoritative voices echoed through the main chamber, and I collapsed on my butt with relief. Kylie had succeeded. Everything was going to be okay. I took my first full breath since I'd agreed to this crazy rescue plan.

A slice of nullifying wood and earth cut through my ward as if it were a child's creation. The backlash rattled my brain in my skull.

"Bloody kludde and their useless handlers!" Walter

cursed. He raced around the corner of the nook and skidded to a stop. "You!" The limp hatchling flopped in Walter's left hand, and it was impossible to tell if he lived. In Walter's right was a glossy black crossbow that pointed unerringly at my chest. My head went light on my shoulders, the tip of the arrow filling my vision.

Walter scanned the ground. "Where are the hatchlings?"

"I . . . I don't know—" I stopped speaking on a squeak when Walter slid his finger to the trigger. Too late, I thought to shout for help. Not that anyone would hear me. I couldn't see the ceremony room from my position, but it sounded like the fighting had doubled despite the guards' arrival. Or because of it. Even if the guards could have heard me, they couldn't react faster than an arrow.

"Where are they?" Walter barked.

Not waiting for my answer, he formed a complicated spike of woven magic. When he released it, the tip flipped left and pierced my ward, disintegrating it. Walter's smile was cold. He flicked a sphere of light into the space near my satchel. With the crossbow never wavering from my chest, he dropped the limp hatchling to the stone floor, bent, and flipped open the top of the satchel. The cygnet snapped at him, and he jerked back, flipping the top closed again.

Helplessly, I watched him grasp the handle, fury and fear pounding in my bloodstream. He turned, hefting the satchel, and centered me in the crossbow's sights.

"Nice try, thief," he said.

My insides coated with ice. "Please—"

From behind the satchel, the dragon hatchling launched. He bit down on Walter's wrist, crushing bone in his rock jaws. Walter screamed and jerked. The crossbow fired. Plaster shards splintered into my face, the arrow missing me by less than a foot. I lurched into Walter. He slammed against the wall, bag and bow falling when he tried to catch himself. Recovering, he swung his left arm at me. The attached hatchling came with it. I ducked too late, and the dragon smashed into my raised forearm and head, knocking me back into the opposite wall. The hatchling dropped to the ground, stunned.

Walter and I stared at the healed hatchling.

"Drop your weapon!" a voice shouted from the mouth of the alcove, still out of sight but loud enough to penetrate my deafened eardrums.

Walter's gaze darted from the healed hatchling to his bow to the satchel.

"No," I cried, pushing from the wall. I tackled him, and we both went down. Walter kicked my thigh, and it went numb. I landed a punch to his gut; then his elbow glanced off my temple. The world skittered, and when it righted, he was on his feet. Walter tore away yet another illusion, this one from the far end of the storage room. Behind it was a smooth wall, but when Walter hit a disguised switch, a hidden panel slid open.

Walter spun to retrieve the hatchlings. Scrambling forward, I wrapped my body around the satchel and limp lion gargoyle.

"Halt! Terra Haven guard!" Footsteps pounded closer.

With a curse and a final kick to my side, Walter fled, empty-handed.

Two guards rounded the corner, glowballs and trap-springer spells preceding them. There were no weapons in their hands—none were necessary; they were trained in defensive and offensive magic, the kind that could stop an arrow or drop an attacker from across the room.

"Hands where I can see them," the woman said.

My skin tightened as a shield sliced between me and my magic. I stretched my hands up beside my head.

"He ran that way." I pointed with a finger.

The male guard approached with null bands—handcuffs that did the work of the spell currently cloaking me.

Something small and heavy landed on my side, hissing.

"What *is* that?" The guard paused. I raised my head to look down my body. The dragon hatchling snaked up my side to perch on my hip. His tiny mismatched wings were flared and his large square head gaped to show bloodred teeth and tongue. Magic rushed back to me at his touch.

"A gargoyle hatchling," I said. I eased a hand to the satchel and flipped the top open. The cygnet squirmed and hissed at the guards. "Hurry. Walter's escaping."

It took long, agonizing minutes to convince the guards I had nothing to do with the harm inflicted on the cygnet and for them to send guards after Walter. I had little hope they'd catch him after his head start. When I was finally allowed to sit up, I moved immediately for the limp demonstration hatchling they hadn't noticed in the curve of my body. The tiny lion weighed less than Herbert had after being used by the Fire Eaters.

"Whoa, there. What're you doing?" demanded the guard who had been called to the nook while the other two chased Walter.

"Helping him."

"I've got orders to round everyone up. You're coming with me."

I ignored him, gathering the familiar blend of quartz earth and fire, with trace levels of the other three elements, and eased it into the hatchling. A tiny spark within him responded. Tears sprang to my eyes. "I'm so sorry I wasn't faster," I whispered to him, feeding him more energy.

"None of that now," the guard said. He grabbed my elbow and pulled me to my feet. The dragon circled my ankles, tail lashing, but he didn't interfere. The guard picked up my bag, bunching the flap so the hissing mutilated baby swan couldn't bite him, and marched me back to the main room. The dragon followed in a strange bunching lope.

Light blazed from a dozen magical sources. I blinked against the brightness. Guards swarmed the room, collecting evidence, but my gaze was drawn to the still bodies near the door. Two men, one shot through the chest, blood soaking his shirt and pooling on the stones, the other decapitated. I glanced away, my stomach churning. There were six prisoners in the room. Each was confined by magic and metal and separated by space, wards, and guards. All six sets of eyes tracked our progress across the room.

The only way out was past the bodies.

10

The guard's guiding grip shifted to support me when the world went light and fuzzy as we approached the decapitated body.

"Don't look down," he urged.

I locked eyes on the stairwell and let him direct me, floating detached from my own feet. The bitter copper smell of blood yanked me back to my body. Another step and the putrid stench of loosed bowels and raw flesh clogged my nostrils. I gagged.

"Not here!" The guard rushed me forward, and we made it to the stairwell before I threw up. He waited until I finished, then half dragged me up the stairs.

Fresh air hit my face and cleared my head, and I remembered the dying hatchling clutched to my chest for the first time since seeing the bodies. I jerked free of the guard and stopped.

"Keep going," he ordered.

"No. Let me heal it first."

"My orders—"

"Stuff your orders." I was bruised and battered,

exhausted and nauseous; I was in no mood to be bullied.

"Don't make me cuff you."

I ignored the guard and knelt. The dragon hatchling loped toward us. His stubby legs hadn't been able to keep up. I felt a twinge of guilt for having forgotten him, too, but mostly gratitude as my weariness faded with his magical boost. I tumbled a handful of seed crystals from my pocket and focused on the lion hatchling and the magic still leeching from his burned-off limbs.

The cub absorbed seed crystal after seed crystal, devouring my magic. Like Herbert, the cub's four legs and wings had been burned away. Even with the dragon hatchling amplifying my power, my magic was clumsy by the time I got to the lion's fourth leg. The elemental strands quivered with fatigue when I painstakingly finished the final wing. The lion hatchling remained unconscious, but he was resting, not dying.

As I worked, I was vaguely aware of the guard kneeling beside me, watching with rapt curiosity. When I leaned back, I went into freefall; then I was in the guard's arms, supported against his broad chest. The dragon hatchling curled up against my sprawled leg, tucked his nose under his tail, and went to sleep. His magical amplification dropped away, and with it my consciousness. The guard shook me, and I fought against the darkness. *Not yet.*

I reached for the satchel and the final hatchling, but my arm wasn't working right. It felt so good to relax against the man's warm chest. My eyes drifted closed again.

"This looks cozy," a woman said from above me.

"Captain!" The guard shifted and I dropped toward the floor, only to be caught before impact. "Uh, sir. I was just . . . She fainted and I . . . The gargoyle, sir, she healed it," the guard stammered.

There was a commotion behind us; then Kylie was at my elbow. She grinned at me. "I knew you could do it, Mika."

At her heels were two huge gargoyles, one a pony-size onyx and amethyst gryphon, the other a cross between an enormous goat and a winged pit bull, with a body made of spotted green jasper. The temple floor trembled beneath the gargoyles' steps. Their eyes glowed with rage.

The guard's grip on me tightened, and I thought I probably would have been afraid if I hadn't been so tired. The goat-headed pit bull sniffed the air, then bounded on huge rock dog paws down the stairs to the ceremony room. A handful of guards rushed after her.

The gryphon stopped at my feet and thrust her face in mine. Under the scrutiny of those fierce eagle eyes, I found it hard to breathe. Then her attention shifted, first to the unconscious lion in my lap, then to the dragon curled at my leg. When she spotted the scared cygnet, still injured and wrapped in my leather bag, she sat back on her haunches. A small blue-green winged panther slid from under the protection of her wings and landed at her feet, scurrying under the gryphon's belly to peer through her thick legs.

Anya.

"May I assist you?" the gryphon asked. Her voice was soft, completely at odds with her enormous stone body.

It took a moment for my brain to catch up. "Please."

I tried to sit up on my own. The guard lifted me.

A trickle of gargoyle-enhanced magic strengthened my exhausted mind and body. It was different from the feel of the hatchlings' power boosts. This was controlled and refined. With the gryphon's strength guiding my magic, healing the cygnet went quickly. When I finished, the cygnet twined her long stony neck against my arm, then fell asleep draped across my lap.

When I looked up, a pair of healers were kneeling beside me, their body language saying they'd been waiting, and watching, for some time. The gryphon remained rooted at my side while the healers stuffed dry energy cakes down my throat, followed by a pitcher of water. The tender lumps on my head were prodded and my arm was wrapped in a coil of mending wood magic. When the medics gave the okay, the captain walked me through the last two days, starting with Anya finding me in my studio up until I healed the baby lion. Then she made me go through it all again.

She questioned Anya, too, but the baby gargoyle's accounting of the events from the time her siblings were kidnapped was convoluted at best. From what I heard, the captain didn't learn anything useful about Walter. After a few minutes, Anya flew onto the gryphon's back and hid beneath her wings, and I was reminded of how young she was. A few weeks old, and she'd already seen the worst of humanity. It was a wonder she had trusted Kylie and me to help her.

The captain released me a little after dawn, and the gryphon accompanied Kylie, me, and the hatchlings home. Since the rescued hatchlings were all still sleeping, Kylie volunteered to carry the dragon, I cradled the lion, and the gryphon carried the cygnet on her back, holding it in place with her wings. Anya rode with her swan sister.

The trip home was a blur. I had a vague impression of Ms. Zuberrie demanding an explanation for our arrival by guard transport and peppering us with questions about the gargoyles, but Kylie intercepted her. The last thing I remembered was opening the door to the balcony for the gargoyles to use as they desired, then collapsing onto my bed, the lion nestled against my stomach.

11

The sun was setting when I woke. My hand went immediately to the bed in front of me, and finding myself alone, I sat up. My entire body protested. I groaned, stretching cramped arms and fingers. Dirt lay in flakes on my bedspread and sifted to the floor from my pants. My pillowcase was grubby. I grimaced, and not for the first time I wished I could afford self-cleaning sheets and clothes, ones with water and air magic woven into the fibers.

My grumbles were cut short when I noticed the lion perched on my slender bookcase. He was squeezed between a battered copy of *Five Steps to Financial Independence* and a dusty misshapen crystal globe, one of my earliest quartz projects. The cub looked like solid, carved citrine with crystal limbs. He didn't move, and his eyes were flat rock, not glowing.

I was across the room in three strides, pressing my hands to his sides and probing him with the gargoyle magic pattern. Life blazed under my fingertips. The lion woke, thin rock eyelids lifting.

"Oh, I'm sorry," I said, panic receding. He wasn't dead,

just sleeping. I should have guessed that; a dead hatchling couldn't move himself from my bed to the bookcase. He yawned, his rock jaw almost unhinging, then shifted to lie down, chin resting on his clear paws. His eyelids slid closed and he stilled. Already I could see veins of gold spreading through his tiny wings and oversize paws. The strength and adaptability of gargoyles were marvels.

Wonder could overshadow my crustiness for only so long. I peeled off my gritty clothes, tossed them in the hamper, and melted under the stream of hot water in my shower. It was dark outside when I finally dressed and thought to check my message bowl. There were two air-pocket messages, both pulsing red with urgency. I touched the edge of the bowl and activated the first message with a nudge of air and earth.

"Mika Stillwater." My boss's voice swelled from the bubble, each word crisply enunciated. Silvia Jones was a strong earth talent, with only a child's grasp of air element. Crafting any message was a surefire way to irritate her, but she sounded more peeved than normal. My stomach sank. I'd missed a second day of work and hadn't sent a message this time.

"I do not run a charity. You are well aware of the rules. Two days' absence requires a doctor's note and advance notice." I scoffed. *Advance notice for being sick?* "I expect you to bring a doctor's note tomorrow. If this is *inconvenient*, your contract with Jones and Sons will be terminated." The bubble crackled in the air before fizzling out.

I slumped in my worktable chair. If everything had gone according to plan, the freelance medicinal vials would be finished, my handsome paycheck collected, my savings holding a lease at Pinnacle Pentagon, and I'd be delivering my resignation at the month's end. My gaze slid to the gilded box still open atop the coffee table. The red velvet insides that had housed my life savings were bare. Glumly, I reached for the message bowl and activated the other bubble.

"When you sign a contract saying you'll complete a project by a deadline, that is when it's due," Althea's voice snapped through the room. "Your avoidance tactics are juvenile and unprofessional. This is the first and last project you'll do for Blackwell-Zakrzewska. Unless you want a formal mark against you, in reputation and filed with the Terra Haven Business Bureau, you will have the remainder of the vials ready for me by seven tomorrow morning. Do not attempt to stall again."

I slumped farther in the chair. Not only was I going to have to grovel to Silvia, but I'd also just lost my most important client. Even without a formal complaint, there would be no stopping rumors.

"That woman should be begging for your services," Kylie said. She stood in my open balcony doorway, hands on hips, glaring at the message bowl. Her wispy blond hair lifted on the night breeze, and Kylie caught it up with a frustrated gesture and trapped it in a hair tie. "Are her precious vials more important than lives? I think not. Which is exactly what I told her."

"You saw her? Today?"

"Yes. She prissed in here, looking down her nose at me and Ms. Zuberrie, demanding we wake you—"

I groaned. "You should have! Now she's going to slander my name." I covered my face in my hands and braced my elbows on my knees, seeing my dreams crumble behind my eyelids.

"She's the one who deserves to have her reputation

blackened. A healer apprentice who puts more importance on some stupid project than life. Absurd!"

"You still should have woken me."

"Why? So you could tell her yourself that you're not done? You're not, right?"

I shook my head.

"Besides, I don't think I *could* have woken you. You slept through our shouting match right outside your door. Now guess what."

I dropped my hands from my face and sat up. I wasn't in the mood for guessing games. Fortunately, Kylie wasn't patient enough to wait.

"You're looking at the *Terra Haven Chronicle*'s evening-edition front-page author!"

"You sold a story?" I asked, stuffing aside my misery for the moment. This was Kylie's dream. Just because mine was shattered didn't mean I would rob her of her moment.

"Not *a* story. Your story! And the hatchlings'. I hope you don't mind that I quoted you a few times. You're a city hero, Mika! When I told the editor at the *Chronicle* what I had, she bought the exclusive and contracted two follow-up stories. Can you believe it?!"

"Of course I can," I said, privately squirming at the mention of *my* story. "Congratulations, Kylie!"

"Oh! Here—" She ran across the balcony and returned with the *Chronicle*. There I was on the front page, bent over the cygnet, repairing her wing.

"Who took the picture?" I asked, not remembering any photographers.

"You should see your face." She laughed. "You didn't think I would show up empty-handed, did you?"

"You didn't. You brought the guards."

"Nope. I brought the gargoyles."

"How?" I'd been too tired last night to ask how Kylie had convinced the guards.

"I figured that if Anya didn't trust people, she would trust gargoyles. So we found the two you saw. After Anya talked to them, they went to the guards with me. They couldn't dismiss me then. And once the guards saw that huge ward, they stopped dragging their feet and called in backup."

"Just in time, too," I said. "You're the real hero, Kylie. I'd be dead without you. All I did was—"

"Hold that thought," Kylie said. She whipped together threads of air and water, weaving a giant sphere and dropping it over both our heads. At my quizzical look, she said, "Better than memory. It'll catch everything we say. What did you think my follow-up story was going to be, Mika? I've been dying to hear what happened all day, and I know my readers feel the same."

"*Your* readers?"

Kylie winked. "Spill."

I spilled, telling her everything that happened from the moment I'd come face-to-face with the kludde to collapsing in the guard's arms after healing the lion. She bombarded me with questions, drawing out details I'd happily have forgotten. I made sure to emphasize that I hadn't been heroic. I knew how Kylie's imagination worked, and I didn't want her getting carried away.

Kylie waved my words aside. "You saved the hatchlings' lives. *That's* heroic."

"That was nothing more than any earth elemental would have done."

"But—"

"Kylie, I was terrified every step of the way. I shook in my boots when confronted with the kludde. I *froze* when Walter had the crossbow on me. The little dragon has more courage than me."

"Modesty is good, but being blinded by it? Stupid. Mika, you might have been scared out of your wits, but you still went through with the rescue. *You saved the hatchlings' lives.*"

"You would have done the same."

Kylie touched her hands to the edges of the sphere and it contracted to a globe that fit in her hand. With a flick, she sent the spell winging toward her room.

"I couldn't have done the same, Mika," Kylie said. "I don't know anyone else who could, not even another earth elemental. Mika, your specialty is so much more than quartz. Do you hear what I'm saying? Your specialty is healing a magical creature. That's . . . that's downright rare."

"But it's mainly just quartz and fire," I protested.

"You're being obtuse," Kylie said. "Now read my first front-page piece."

Kylie thrust the paper into my hands. I blushed at her opening paragraph: *Last night, a lone woman bravely infiltrated a megalomaniac's lair to rescue three tortured gargoyle hatchlings. Mika Stillwater, an earth elemental and quarry project manager, acted at the behest of two orphan gargoyles, stepping into the role of hero as if she were born to it.*

"Really? This is . . ."

"True," Kylie said.

"Embarrassing. I told you—"

"Oh, hush. Read."

Kylie filled in the backstory, highlighting Herbert's rescue and the atrocities he'd endured. There was a good deal about the guards' actions—the unit who broke Walter's ward, their strategic capture of the kludde and its handler, the raid on the temple—but no mention that they hadn't believed me or Kylie without the backing of two adult gargoyles.

Eight people were arrested for attending the illegal auction. The police are tracking down leads on a dozen others. Walter Pratt remains at large, the article concluded.

"They didn't catch him," I said.

Kylie shook her head. "In the confusion, most people got away, though I obviously didn't say that. That wouldn't earn me any favors and it might alarm the public. I went by the station today to see if there was an update. They think Walter's gone to ground. My rumor scouts confirm it. There hasn't been a useful peep about him."

"He really liked having the power," I said, remembering Walter's expression of triumphant superiority when he created the enormous ward that rocked us all. "He's not going to stop."

"I don't think so, either. Look at how many people showed up for the auction. He was going to make a fortune."

"Speaking of money . . . Any word on getting my—our—money back from what the police confiscated from the kludde handler?"

"I think that's the last thing on their mind," Kylie said. She patted my arm; I didn't feel consoled. My final hope to salvage my career imploded.

Her gaze went to the lion on my bookcase. "How's he doing?"

"Good. Sleeping." I wanted to curl up on my bed and savor the oncoming depression, but that would be unchari-table. Not to mention counterproductive. I still needed to finish Althea's project before I headed off to work tomorrow. But first: "Are the two adult gargoyles still here?"

"They went home this morning."

"Oh." I hadn't had a chance to thank them or to explain

that I hadn't been trying to overstep my abilities by being the one to heal the hatchlings rather than searching for someone stronger. "Did the other hatchlings go with them?"

"Nope. They're all still here." Kylie grinned and bounced on her toes. "Four gargoyles, even if they are very small, lined up on a house full of nobodies has created quite a stir in the neighborhood. Ms. Zuberrie acts like she was put out by all the visitors we've had today—it's been nonstop, Mika; everyone found an excuse to drop in—but you can tell she's never been happier."

I grinned back. Holding court must have thrilled Ms. Zuberrie to her toes.

Kylie followed me out to the balcony. The hatchlings were outlined against the twilit sky, all four in a tight clump close to the balcony edge. Four pair of glowing eyes watched us. Everyone looked okay. I felt an unexpected swell of pride.

The dragon spread his crimson-veined crystal wings and launched straight at me. I caught him and staggered back against the wall, my arms straining under twenty pounds of wriggling rock. Bracing his front paws on my chest, hind paws on my palms, he put his square, stone-bearded face in mine and, very precisely, enunciated, "Thank you."

His voice carried an undercurrent of chimes.

"You're welcome," I said. A flash popped, blinding me. The gargoyle jerked from my arms and flapped to the balcony railing, growling at Kylie.

"That'll look great with the next article," she said, unapologetic.

I wasn't sure what would happen next. I didn't have any experience with baby gargoyles, or gargoyles of any kind. "Um. You guys are welcome to stay here as long as you want," I told the hatchlings. "Or to go, if that's what you want . . ."

The dragon flew to the bookcase, landing on the shelf beside the lion and knocking several books and knickknacks to the floor. The cub opened an eye, saw the dragon, and closed it. Herbert flew to my worktable. The cygnet stretched her wings, then folded her head under one and went to sleep. Anya closed her eyes, too.

I glanced at Kylie, and she shrugged.

"I guess they're staying. I need to get writing," she said. "I've got an article due tomorrow." She danced in place, then left, singing.

"And I need to finish the vials," I told the room at large, settling into my work chair.

Herbert picked up a seed crystal, tossed it to the back of his mouth, and swallowed it. His eyes bulged. He hunched forward, and with a loud, wet hacking sound, threw up. The crystal landed in a slimy puddle and rolled across my worktable.

12

After the last few days' excitement, it was unfair to rise with dawn, dress in dull work attire, and trudge down to breakfast, only to be intercepted by Althea in the foyer. Stifling a sigh, I summoned a smile.

"I see your friend's description of your 'condition' was an exaggeration," she said.

"Have you been waiting long?" I asked, wondering how I'd missed the bell chime.

"Three days too long, Mika Stillwater."

I winced. I'd walked right into that one.

"Let me just—"

"Your lack of professionalism is appalling. I am a forgiving person—"

I gaped at the lie.

"—otherwise I'd see you never worked in this city again. It's not as if your services are unique," Althea said. "There are a hundred other earth elementals in the city who can do what you do."

My spine snapped straight. "If that were so, you would

have contracted through someone else," I said, shocked by my boldness even as I spoke.

Althea's face pinched tighter. "Quality is of no use to me if it is to the detriment of punctuality."

How long had she been waiting to use that line? "If you'll just wait—"

"I am through waiting!"

"—here," I continued, speaking over her. "I will return with your vials, Althea Stoneward."

She clamped her mouth shut, affronted I'd used her full name as if she were an apprentice under my authority. I turned away before she could see me smile. Feeling a little more perky, I trotted back upstairs. I would be delighted to see the last of Althea.

I was three steps into my room before a prickling sensation on my neck registered. I glanced around, and adrenaline spurted through me. The lion and dragon were imprisoned on my bookcase in cages of crackling destructive magic. The dragon twisted in panic, but the lion stared behind me, wide eyes affixed.

Dread loosened my body, and I spun toward my bed. Lying, hands clasped behind his head, muddy boots crossed at the ankle atop my pillow, was Walter Pratt.

"Hello, Hero Stillwater," Walter said, rolling to his feet.

"How did you find—" No, I knew the answer to that question. The article in the paper. "How did you get in here?"

"I see you've restored the hatchlings. Very useful," he said. "Opens up a world of possibilities."

He was only a fraction taller than me and similar in build. There should have been nothing terrifying about him, with his sandy-haired, boy-next-door looks. But up close, I could see madness in his green eyes. The open door was just three steps away, the balcony a little farther. A shout would echo downstairs and also reach Kylie's room, if she was there.

Walter flicked a hand, and a blast of air closed the door. I jumped, eyes darting to the balcony, but Walter shifted to block that escape. He tossed a handful of objects at me. I flinched and ducked, instinct restoring movement to limbs I'd forgotten existed. I grabbed for air, fashioning a deflective shield even as the items clattered around my feet. I glanced down. Over a dozen seed crystals rolled chaotically before snapping into a perfect circle around me. Walter engaged the crystals.

A blanket of magic smothered me, bearing down as if to flatten me. My neck strained, my spine compressed. I collapsed to my hands and knees. The pressure eased, allowing me to twist to look up at Walter.

"Much better, Mika." His smile chased ice through my veins, jolting me from my stupor. I grabbed for magic. It trickled to me, warped and weak from the swirl of wood, fire, and air that trapped me. I was no match for Walter's power, and we both knew it.

"You and I will make a great team," Walter said.

I screamed, finding my voice at last. "Help! Kylie! Help!"

Walter cocked his head to the side and cupped his ear; bruises circled his left wrist from the dragon's bite. "What's that, Mika? Did you say something?"

My stomach sank. I screamed again, wordless frustration and fear unleashed into a sound-consuming void. Walter was one step ahead of me, again.

"Tsk-tsk, Mika. Don't interrupt. I'm annoyed with you. Do you know how long it took to set up last night's auction? And then you ruined it all. I could happily kill you for that."

I kicked a crystal with a booted foot. Pain convulsed up

my heel, through my ankle, my knee, my hip, vibrating
through every joint and muscle of my body. When it
receded, I was lying on my side, knees curled to my chest.
Walter's feet were in my line of sight. He was standing at my
worktable.

"You have some skill," he said, holding out one of the
vials I had finished last night. "Such delicate work." He
dropped it. The vial shattered against the floor in a musical
tinkling of paper-thin crystal. "Each one as perfect as the
last," he mused, selecting another and dropping it. Shards
sparkled across the hardwood floor.

"Stop," I said. It came out soft, pathetic, breathless. I
rolled to my knees. The cage had constricted, but I squished
under it, refusing to remain vulnerable on my side. "Stop!" I
shouted. I couldn't lift my head to see above Walter's thighs.
Another vial fragmented against the floor. "Stop it, you sick
bastard!"

I stared at the shards of my labor and welcomed the
surge of anger. It helped me think. Walter had trapped me
in a net just as he had trapped the gargoyles. I'd removed
the nets at the temple; I could remove this one. I wasn't a
helpless hatchling. I was an earth practitioner. No one was
going to bind me with quartz.

I probed the seed crystal in front of me. A whirlwind of
wood and fire and air suffocated the trickle of magic I held in
a feeble grasp. Doing my best to ignore Walter while simulta-
neously appearing to be doing nothing more than hanging
on his every word, I relaxed into the chaotic energy, searching
for a pattern. Four times, it knocked me out of its weave, my
dribble of magic buffeted by the raw power of Walter's
creation. On the fifth try, I found a weak link at a seed crystal
where the magic funneled through narrow bands.

"Your death, however satisfying that might be," Walter continued, "is a shortsighted goal at best." A vial crashed to the floor. "Your abilities are too valuable. With you, there is no limit. I can sell the hatchlings a hundred times, and when they're returned, useless, you will repair them. It's a beautiful cycle, Mika."

Bile washed up my throat. Walter didn't respect the lives of the magical creatures, and he certainly didn't value my life. He viewed the hatchlings and me only in terms of his monetary and magical gain. But I wasn't going to be a victim and neither were the hatchlings.

I cut the flow of power from the first seed crystal. It rolled an inch toward me, unfettered by the binds of the spell. I prayed Walter wasn't paying attention and focused on the next crystal. It took three more severed links before I felt a difference in the level of magic I could pull. I worked even faster, snapping the locks on my cage with increased efficiency.

"FSPPs will look *average* compared to me. Full-five companies will beg for my services." Walter laughed.

Eight of the fifteen seed crystals were disconnected, and the prison holding me cracked into a semicircle of wild magic. Walter whirled from the table in shock.

I scrambled away from the snapping current of power. Walter shoved the freed crystals toward me with a blast of air. I was ready this time. I opened myself wide to raw power. Hundreds of hours working with quartz made it easy to resonate my magic with the seed crystals hurtling through the air. I thrust my power through each crystal, claiming and stacking them in a line across the floor at my feet, forming a half-inch wall between Walter and myself. At the last second, I felt the seed crystals at my back lift and spin in my direction, dragging the deadly, uncontrolled magic with them.

13

I sidestepped, crashing into my coffee table. Dividing my focus, I held the clean crystals at my feet and pressed destructive elements into the hazardous seeds still in Walter's control. I worked faster than ever before, breaking the links between Walter's erratic net and each crystal while it was still in the air. Walter's unfettered magic flared out of control, scorching a flat line in the bathroom wall before extinguishing. The empty crystals clattered to the floor and scattered.

"You can't win this fight," Walter said. "You're hardly a medium spectrum, and I'm so much more."

It was true. That didn't mean I had to give up, though.

"Kylie! Guards!" I yelled. As I predicted, Walter launched an air net to catch the sound, and that gained me precious seconds. I jammed earth magic through the scattered crystals, aligning them with the seven in my control. With a shove of blunt earth element, I grew them together in a single rod. Just as fast, I severed the crystal in four places, making five bars of quartz, each as long as my palm. With a blast of air, I knocked them toward Walter. If I could get them around him, it would make a far stronger cage than the string of seed crystals—

Walter threw up a wall of air, blocking the crystal. "Ah, ah, ah," he said, shaking a finger at me. He increased the push of air, and I strained to hold the quartz bars in place. The brilliance of my spontaneous plan betrayed me as Walter turned it against me.

Walter grinned and added an ounce more of air, toying with me. The crystal bars inched closer. In a head-to-head challenge, Walter's magic eclipsed mine, and I'd lost my advantage of surprise.

At Walter's feet, a handful of crystal shards shifted in our elemental battle. I almost dropped my weave of air when I *felt* those shards move. In straining to force the quartz bars around Walter, I'd left myself wide open to all quartz, and even broken, the residue of my magic in the shattered, fragile quartz responded. The beginning of a crazy plan formed.

I pulled a trickle of magic from the wall of air holding the crystal bars at bay. They jumped three inches toward me before I slowed them to a slide again. Walter barked a laugh.

"Give up now, Mika, and come with me. You know it's inevitable."

In two feet, the crystal bars would trap me, and Walter was eroding that distance with alarming speed. Panicking seemed like a good option, but I smothered the urge.

Only my extensive work with quartz enabled me to quest with a feeler of earth magic through the shards while most of my attention remained on the air struggle between us. I directed magic through the brittle scraps beneath and around Walter's booted feet, connecting each fragment into a complex web. As the crystal bars slid another hand span toward me, I expanded the linked network of earth magic, at first as large as Walter's feet, then as wide as his shoulders.

Sweat slid down my spine and beaded on my forehead. Walter's magic shifted, earth twining into the crystal bars. He was setting the net again, and I knew, ironically, I wouldn't escape from the anchors I'd created. With a cry, I shifted my push on air to a pull, and the crystal bars shot past me. I slammed my full strength into the web of earth beneath Walter.

Wood, air, and fire spiraled and snapped in a containment field Walter had taught me. Only, instead of forming a circular cage of power, individual lines of binding magic arced from each shard, forming a bundle of ropes. Each rope unfurled and snaked to Walter, knotting around his legs.

Walter countered, slicing at the bonds with destructive magic faster than I'd cut his anchors. I didn't stop him. Instead, I spread the net wider and wider, through the fragments on the table and under the table, and scattered a yard in every direction. We were working with quartz, my specialty; even though Walter had more strength, he couldn't match my speed or dexterity. He severed a dozen anchors while I grew thirty more. Cables of magic climbed his body, grappling his wrists, his torso, his neck, his ears, thumbs, and belt loops. Each strand cut through Walter's magic, weakening him until he was unable to sever the smallest of my anchors. I didn't stop, though. I wove the net through every shard and fragment until Walter was ensnared in a woven cocoon of magic, immobilized except for his eyes. Not even his mouth could open with the snarl of magic wrapping his jaw shut.

The trap was erratic at best, since the shards were scattered haphazardly around the room. If I let my hold slacken even a fraction, I knew Walter would find a way to wiggle free.

Casting about the room, I saw the crystal bars. One was at my feet, and I belatedly felt the sting of where it had slammed into my shin. The other four were against the bathroom wall. Not daring to pull a drop of magic from the net, I gathered the bars with my hands and placed them evenly around Walter and the shards, squeezing behind my worktable and pushing aside my coffee table until I had an approximation of a circle. It took extreme dexterity to weave the frayed ends of the modified trap into the crystal bars while maintaining magic through hundreds of irregular fragments. I didn't stop until all the shards were tied off and each crystal bar reinforced. I looked for weak links like I'd exploited in Walter's trap, finding none. With numb pride, I stepped back and examined my work.

It was . . . beautiful. Every line of magic glimmered with broken refractions of light from its shard of origin, giving Walter the illusion of being swathed in spun crystal.

A muffled whimper made me turn. The hatchlings! I stumbled to the bookcase and demolished the cages holding them. With all my practice and Walter's magic weakened by my trap, it was easy. I threw open the balcony door and darted outside. On the railing, Anya, Herbert, and the cygnet were ensnared together. I disbursed Walter's sinister magic cage and rushed back into my room to check on my prisoner.

"Mika! Are you okay?" Kylie gripped the balcony railing, eyes darting from me to Walter.

At the sight of her, my adrenaline crashed, and the world blackened, swirled with excessive color. I dropped to the floor, my legs collapsing beneath me.

"Mika!"

Kylie was at my side, supporting me against her body. "Is that Walter?" she asked.

I nodded, the movement taxing my exhausted body.

"I'm through waiting, Mika Stillwa—" Althea burst into the room and stopped in her tracks. "Wha-what is . . . Who is . . . Mika?"

The kernel of compassion that had led Althea to Black-well-Zakrzewska kicked in, and the apprentice healer crossed the room to press her hands to my temple. A cool wash of magic slid across my skin, giving me a measure of strength.

"What is going on here?" she demanded.

Feet pounded on the stairs, and we all turned toward the commotion in the doorway.

14

"I run a proper house," Ms. Zuberrie protested. "Who do you think holds the blight at bay on this block? Where were you last year when those heathens were burning the tops off all the trees on this street? I could have used a squad then."

Three guards, linked and magic primed, stacked up at the door. Two more fell in line behind them. Althea shrieked and cowered behind me. Kylie clutched my hand. Behind the guards, I could just see Ms. Zuberrie's white-blond head craning to peer over the guards' backs.

The guards scanned the room with eyes that missed nothing and showed no surprise at Walter's frozen form. In head to toe gray, the only markings on the five were small elemental symbols on their stiff collars, one guard for each element. No ordinary guards, these were a full-five squad, elite guards trained to work as a unit against extreme threats like full-five militia groups and rampaging magical creatures. They converged on my tiny apartment.

With practiced efficiency, Terra Haven's most deadly warriors swarmed through my studio—not pausing at the sight of the traumatized hatchling gargoyles clinging to the railing. Two crossed the balcony and disappeared into Kylie's room. The wood elemental remained at the door, his tall frame blocking Ms. Zuberrie. Moments later, they reconvened, magic relaxed and link dissipated. The water and earth elementals—a slender woman with copper hair and a tall woman I'd mistaken for a man at first—moved to the far side of my worktable, studying Walter. The fire and air elementals, two men cut from the same broad, unyielding cloth, stood between my bed and the coffee table, looming over where Kylie, Althea, and I crouched. The giant wood elemental managed to make the two burly guards look diminutive when he stepped fully into the room.

"See, I told you nothing was wrong," Ms. Zuberrie said. "Mika's a good girl. She wouldn't . . ." Ms. Zuberrie clutched the door frame, her eyes riveted on Walter. But my landlady was nothing if not resilient, and she recovered with remarkable speed. "Mika, just what is going on here?" she demanded, marching into my room. She made it two steps; there simply wasn't any more space in my studio apartment.

"Ma'am, we'll take it from here," the air elemental said in a deep voice.

"That's good to know," Ms. Zuberrie said, "but I'll not be going anywhere. This is my establishment." She gave the guard her sternest glare, which he ignored.

"I . . . I have nothing to do with"—Althea flapped a hand toward the network of magic squeezing Walter—"with *that*." She stood, puffing her chest and looking down her nose at me. "Mika, consider our—"

"Ma'am, please go with Officer Marciano. We'll need your statement," the air guard said, cutting off Althea's haughty speech.

"I really don't have time—"

"We appreciate your cooperation," the wood giant Marciano said, his quiet, authoritative voice ending Althea's protests. He guided the healer apprentice from the room with one large hand on her back, sweeping Ms. Zuberrie along with them. The loss of three people made my apartment almost breathable again.

Kylie and I scrambled to our feet. Standing didn't lessen my growing claustrophobia. The dragon leapt from the bookcase to my chest, and Kylie braced my back while he clambered to my shoulders, getting tangled in my long hair. Wincing, I gathered my hair and planted my feet to balance the extra twenty pounds of rock wrapped around my neck.

"Who can explain what happened here?" the fire elemental demanded. He had dark blue eyes, a five o'clock shadow at eight in the morning, and a jaw that could bench press twice my body weight.

"Ah, that's Walter Pratt," I said.

"And you are?" asked the air elemental. His brown eyes were bracketed with crow's-feet, and some silver lightened his brown hair. I found it much easier to talk to him than the fire elemental.

"I'm Mika Stillwater."

"Kylie Grayson," Kylie said, holding out her hand. The air elemental smiled a fraction and shook her hand. "I'm so pleased with how quickly you responded. Can you tell me who tipped you off to Walter's intentions?"

"She sounds like a reporter," the fire elemental growled.

"Do you know who Walter Pratt is, Guard . . . ?" Kylie let the question trail off.

"It's Captain Monaghan," the air elemental said. "And, yes, we're well aware of Mr. Pratt. I'd like to know who bound Pratt."

I could feel Kylie gather herself to speak, so I cut in. "I did, sir."

"Just you?" the fire elemental demanded.

"Yes, sir."

The squad members exchanged glances. Kylie couldn't let the silence rest.

"Captain Monaghan, can you explain how you learned of Pratt's presence in Mika's room?"

"Velasquez, please escort Ms. Grayson to her rooms and take her statement," the captain said.

"Ms. Grayson." The fire elemental motioned for Kylie to precede him from the room.

"Winnigan, check the rooms across the hall, then assist Marciano," Captain Monaghan said, addressing the redhead water elemental. He turned to the earth elemental. "Seradon, what do you—"

"Sir, I think I should stay." Kylie faced the captain, ignoring Velasquez's outstretched hand.

"Ma'am, it would be best if you returned to your rooms—"

"Let me put it this way, Captain," Kylie interrupted. "I'm not leaving Mika's side unless I'm carried out."

Velasquez twitched in Kylie's direction, then crossed his arms and settled back on his heels at a gesture from the captain. I felt a wash of gratitude for Kylie's loyalty and support, even if she was partially motivated by her quest for a story.

"Very well, Ms. Grayson. But"—he held up a hand when Kylie opened her mouth—"you must remain silent."

Kylie crossed her arms and pinched her lips in an unconscious mimicry of Velasquez's posture. It wasn't nearly as intimidating on Kylie's slender frame.

The guards shuffled aside for Winnigan, the water

elemental, to squeeze past and exit the apartment. With six people—one frozen and two men whose presence took up twice as much room as their extra-large bodies—my apartment felt short on air.

"Walk me through what happened here," Monaghan said. He pulled a record bauble from his pocket and activated it with a brush of air magic. Kylie mimicked him, though she didn't have the high-tech bauble to focus her magic on and instead had to hold a sphere of air while I talked. Monaghan's expression tightened, but he didn't say anything and Velasquez only growled once.

I started with Kylie's article in the paper, then stammered my way through the explanation of Walter's attack. Monaghan listened without interrupting. I did my best to ignore Velasquez, who did a phenomenal impression of a grumpy gargoyle. Seradon, the earth elemental, continued to examine Walter as I talked, but she cast frequent glances at the hatchlings.

"Pratt is a stronger elemental than you," Monaghan said when I finished. "At best, you're a medium spectrum. He's nearly a full spectrum. How is it that you were able to overpower him?"

I stared at Walter's cocooned body. "I didn't. I mean, I couldn't overpower him, but I was faster. I have a knack for quartz."

"I'll say," Seradon muttered.

"You said you learned how to do this"—the captain tipped his head toward Walter—"from Pratt, but this isn't his MO. I've never seen anything like it."

"I modified Walter's trap."

"Spur of the moment, in the middle of your struggle with Pratt." Captain Monaghan made it sound like an accusation.

"Through jagged quartz," Seradon added.

I nodded.

"Mika's got more skill with quartz in her pinkie than most full-spectrum earth elementals have in their entire body," Kylie said.

The squad members let that ride.

"Is it true that you healed the hatchlings?" Seradon asked. She moved closer to peer at the dragon, but she never put her back to Walter.

"Mika's a gargoyle healer," Kylie confirmed.

"I just used quartz to heal their burned-off limbs," I said, uncomfortable with accepting the label of *healer* when I didn't know what I was doing.

"No. I could just heal limbs," Seradon said, holding the dragon's paw. He nuzzled her hand. "You regrew and . . . knit them back together." The dragon trilled. Seradon stepped back and refocused on me. "I've never met a healer who wasn't full-spectrum before. Of course, I've never met a midlevel earth elemental who could work such complex magic."

"I can't. I mean, it's only with quartz. It's my specialty."

"A full-spectrum pentacle potential–strength specialty," Seradon mused. "That's a new one, too, but I don't have another explanation."

Captain Monaghan wasn't convinced and made me demonstrate the net I'd used to ensnare Walter on a free shard. By the time I finished, Winnigan had returned to crowd the room.

The captain finally turned to Kylie, who was bouncing on her toes to restrain her questions. "You asked me how we knew to come," he said. "We've been tracking Walter for two weeks, and the night of the auction, we were able to identify his magical fingerprint, so to speak. When he started throwing his magic around here, we mobilized."

Kylie blurted out several more questions, but I didn't listen. I kept replaying FSPP Seradon's compliments and confirmation that I was a gargoyle healer. When the captain addressed me again, he had to repeat himself before I noticed.

"Can you undo it? I think we've let Walter stew long enough, Ms. Stillwater."

"Uh." I eyed the tangled mess of earth and wood and fire. I was tempted to say no and let Seradon unravel it, but when Kylie gave me an encouraging nod, I knew I had to at least try.

I stepped away from Kylie and closer to Walter. Seradon circled around the far side of the table to stand behind Walter. Velasquez, the fire elemental, shifted to stand behind me, forcing Kylie to move back near the door. Winnigan and Monaghan moved to ring Walter. I felt the readiness in the squad—to apprehend Walter, but just as likely to control any backlash of magic that got away from me.

There was a flurry at the balcony door. Anya, Herbert, and the cygnet careened into the room. Anya dropped to the captain's feet, Herbert landed on a clean edge of my worktable, and the cygnet alighted on Velasquez's shoulder, buffeting his head with her crystalline wings. The fire elemental cursed and steadied the hatchling, then glared at me. I looked away before he caught my smile.

All mirth died when I stared at Walter. He was facing me, hate burning in his eyes. Taking a deep breath, I reached for my magic. It came in a gargoyle-enhanced rush. Working on what I'd learned when I'd destroyed Walter's traps, I unraveled the larger strands of magic from the crystal bars, feeding the destructive magic into each shard at the source. The anchors released like unsnapped buttons, quick and efficient. This wasn't Walter's magic; it was my own, and it responded with gratifying alacrity. Still, even after the bars were removed, there were hundreds more anchors, and it was at least ten minutes before I felt the weave holding Walter weaken.

Suddenly Velasquez lifted me and deposited me behind him. I yelped and dropped my magic. The squad ignored me. As a unit, they converged on Walter, who was fighting free of the remaining bonds. For a second, Walter's magic flared, hot and bright, and then the squad snapped null cuffs to his wrists and plucked the bow from his waist.

"It was all her!" Walter shouted. "She primed the auction. She stole the hatchlings. I had nothing to do with it. She was holding me captive. Arrest her! She's—"

The cygnet launched from Velasquez's shoulder, her clawed lion's feet slashing toward Walter's face. He screamed in terror.

Velasquez plucked the hatchling from the air, opened a window, and gently tossed her out. She squeaked and flapped around the bay windows to the balcony door, angling for Walter again, only to be brought up short by Anya's hiss. Squawking her disappointment, the cygnet landed on the captain's head, purple-veined crystal feathers ruffled. Even Velasquez smiled at the sight.

15

"**C**heck it out," Kylie said, slapping down the *Terra Haven Chronicle* onto my desk.

I rolled the final vial into a cloth and slid it into the pouch with the others. When I glanced up, I groaned.

"Gargoyle Healer Mika Stillwater Instrumental in Capturing Felon" was typed in boulder-size letters across the top of the page. Below it was a picture of Walter being dragged down Ms. Zuberrie's front steps by the full-five squad, with me framed in the doorway, the dragon hatchling standing on two legs on my shoulder.

"Did you see the byline?"

"Kylie, I saw you race ahead of the squad to take the picture," I said. She planted her fists on her hips and pouted. "Congratulations on getting another front-page story. But really? *Instrumental*?" I wasn't sure how I felt about the bold letters proclaiming me to be a gargoyle healer, either. I had the potential, but I still had a lot to learn. I would have said "fledgling healer" or "healer in training." Or better yet, I wouldn't have mentioned me at all.

"Don't be modest, Mika. It's no fun. Now read!"

She spread the paper open and moved the bag of vials to the coffee table. Herbert cracked an eye at us, then curled up tighter on the edge of my table in the sunbeam. His limbs were still mostly translucent crystal, but the veins of rose quartz and blue dumortierite were longer, reaching nearly to the tips of his wings and down to his toes. The other hatchlings were healing, too, and none seemed slowed by their crystal limbs in the meantime. Even the lion was outside today, perched on the eaves.

"You're not reading," Kylie said.

I read. I squirmed through the parts that mentioned me, feeling that Kylie exaggerated my actions in the events, but her depiction of the full-five squad was dead-on. Reading about Walter's imprisonment filled me with a sense of triumph all over again.

"The managing editor has already hired me to cover Walter's trial. Depending on how that goes, I could be taken on as staff. Isn't that great?"

"You'll be running that paper in a year," I said, believing it.

Kylie glowed. "What about you? What are you going to do?"

"Not work for Silvia Jones," I said.

"You quit! Good for you."

"Actually, she fired me."

"What!"

"She sent a message this morning. Said she didn't need someone with my 'reputation' in her office. Something about Jones and Sons not employing people who 'fraternize with criminals.' She also accused me of having a second job that was, and again I quote, 'interfering with my performance and attendance at Jones and Sons and a direct violation of my employment contract.' At least she'll be sending my final check today."

"That woman has no business sense. She would be lucky to get someone with your reputation in her office. Good riddance!"

I smiled. I should have been overjoyed to never return to Jones and Sons, to never have to suffer another lecture from Silvia or be condescended to by her sons again, but I was really going to miss the steady paychecks. Without my savings, even with Althea's reduced payment for the remaining vials, I barely had enough to buy groceries after this month's rent.

"Now you can concentrate on running your business," Kylie said.

"My savings are gone, Kylie. I can't run a business while I have no money."

"Throw away that five-year plan, Mika, and just leap in. Work for yourself full-time."

"In the meantime, Ms. Zuberrie will evict me."

Kylie snorted. "Evict the city hero? Hardly. She's loving all the attention of having you here. Plus, if you leave, so will the gargoyles, and she's not giving that up. Her cleaning spells have double their usual strength. You should see the kitchen: the tan floor tiles are white now."

"My shop at the Pinnacle Pentagon has already been leased. I can't work from here—"

"What have you been doing for the last three years?" Kylie asked.

"That was different. Maybe if I took another quarry job . . ." I trailed off as Kylie crouched and peered under my bed. "What are you doing?"

"Looking for Mika."

"What?"

"My friend doesn't just give up, so I know you're an impostor."

"I'm not giving up! I'm being prac—"

"If you say you're being practical, I'm going to hurt you."

"What would you have me do? Live paycheck to paycheck?"

"Why not? It won't be forever."

I glared at Kylie. It was easy for her to be optimistic. She was riding high from landing her dream job, and she had paychecks coming her way. I had nothing: no clients, no job, no money, no prospects. In three days, my dreams had plummeted from attainable to impossible.

My gaze fell on Herbert. *If I could do it all over again, would I do anything differently?* The answer was immediate: of course not.

I took a deep breath and pushed aside self-pity. "At least we'll still be neighbors," I said, meeting Kylie's blue eyes.

"And you won't turn into a snob living in that hoity-toity neighborhood," Kylie agreed.

"And my apartment has more gargoyles than the Pinnacle does."

Kylie grinned. "You could charge more, too, as a gargoyle-enhanced practitioner."

I grinned back. This was starting to sound like it might work. "And who knows what sort of business your article will generate for me."

"I bet you have people lined up at the door."

As if in response, the front doorbell chimed.

"That'll be Althea," I said. I grabbed the swaddled bundle of vials and headed for the stairs, Kylie trailing behind me.

Althea waited in the foyer, lips pursed, nose in the air, though her shifting eyes and startled jerks at every sound coming from the kitchen spoiled her aloof airs. I wondered if she was looking for gargoyles or criminals or maybe the full-five squad to come barreling out of the dining room. Nervous or not, she inspected each vial before handing over my payment. She was just turning to leave when the door sprang open and a harried woman rushed in. Her silk clothes were rumpled and her hair had fallen from its chignon, but there was no mistaking the FSPP status in her bearing. Two boys trotted in behind her, both in their teens.

"Ms. Gideon!" Althea said, clearly shocked to see the FSPP on my doorstep.

"Althea Stoneward? I wouldn't think you'd need a gargoyle healer," the woman said, her gaze darting between me and the healer apprentice.

"I am here on business for Blackwell-Zakrzewska—" Althea's eyes widened and she clamped her mouth shut. I smiled. In her attempt to make herself seem more important, Althea had just endorsed my skills to an FSPP.

"If you or Blackwell-Zakrzewska have any further need of someone skilled with quartz, Althea, please keep me in mind," I said, making the most of the situation. Althea scowled at me before bidding the FSPP good-bye. When the door slammed behind her, Ms. Gideon's words sank in.

"Are you Mika Stillwater?" Ms. Gideon asked.

I nodded, my tongue stuck to the roof of my mouth.

"Good. We need your help." She gestured, and her oldest son stepped forward, a small gargoyle in his arms. The upper half of her body was a dog's head, torso, and front legs; the lower half was the tail end of a sea horse, including a sea horse's delicate fin-wings. Her entire body was composed of intricate swirls of black, gray, and red agate. The gargoyle's gray eyes were dull and her face pinched.

"Um, I'm not really—" *trained for this,* I was going to finish, but Kylie cut me off.

"Right this way," she said, gesturing toward the living room. The boy thrust the gargoyle into my arms and everyone marched expectantly after Kylie. I staggered behind them, excuses forming in my head. The gargoyle weighed at least forty pounds, and I sank to the floor before I dropped her. Large puppy eyes blinked at me, and then the gargoyle relaxed in my arms, completely trusting. I met Kylie's gaze, then Ms. Gideon's.

"I'm willing to pay whatever it takes," Ms. Gideon said.

"Oh, that's not—"

"I'd be happy to discuss Mika's fees while she works," Kylie said. Kylie drew the FSPP to the side of the room, away from me. Ms. Gideon's oldest son followed, but the younger one knelt across from me.

"Can you help Aretha?" he asked, his voice cracking over the words.

I looked away from his hopeful expression and into the soulful eyes of the gargoyle.

I'd spent a lifetime honing my quartz skills to prove I was better than average, to prove that I was good enough to compete with FSPPs and worthy of others' respect. I'd never dreamed that those skills would translate into something far more important: saving lives. I felt a rush of pride at the thought; I was a gargoyle healer.

"Yes. I can help."

What's next for Mika and the gargoyles?

_____

Read on for a sneak peek from
REBECCA CHASTAIN'S
next Gargoyle Guardian Chronicles novel.

_____

AVAILABLE NOW!

CURSE OF THE GARGOYLES
SNEAK PEEK

GARGOYLE GUARDIAN CHRONICLES BOOK 2

"How's Oliver doing, Mika?" Kylie asked.

I jerked and glanced up from the journal open across my lap. We sat outside at a bustling café, soaking in the afternoon sun, and while I'd started out focused on double-checking my notes about my latest patient, a prasiolite and onyx gargoyle who had ingested moldy quartz loam, I'd long since stopped seeing the words. Instead, I'd been idly spinning a pentagram of the five elements above the pages, tuning them to perfect harmony with Oliver.

"Should I get another coffee?" Kylie asked, indicating her empty cup.

"Let me check." We'd been here a little over an hour. It was probably long enough.

I nudged the pentagram into flight, lifting it above the heads of people in the busy city pentagon before zeroing in on Oliver. The half-grown gargoyle crouched two buildings over and three stories up on his favorite perch on the peak of the library's marble facade, craning his long neck to peer over the edge to watch people come and go. Several government buildings and a few restaurants, including the café, ringed the pentagon, but Oliver preferred the magic of library users. I'd chosen the table where Kylie and I sat partially because it afforded me a view of Oliver at all times, but mostly because it was an outdoor seat close enough for me to reach him with my magic.

The pentagram kissed Oliver's side and dipped into his body. In the past five months, I'd perfected the elemental blend of my gargoyle companion: carnelian quartz earth, with a strong band of fire and smaller portions of wood, water, and air. I tried to be discreet and not disturb him, but he lifted his head to find me even as my magic told me he was feeling balanced and healthy.

"He's better now," I told Kylie. "Between an hour or two a week here and a couple hours at the market, he's stabilizing."

I let the weave dissolve and shut the journal. It'd been a gift from Kylie, and she'd had *Mika Stillwater, Gargoyle Healer* embossed in gold on the leather cover. After all these months, I still got the same nervous thrill at seeing my name and title together. Most of the time I still considered myself a midlevel earth elemental with a specialty in quartz—a specialty that happened to make me uniquely suited to work with the living quartz bodies of gargoyles. I loved my new career as a healer, but I kept expecting someone more powerful and knowledgeable to come along and replace me.

Standing, I hefted my bag filled with twenty-five pounds of seed crystals that I'd purchased earlier and wedged the journal on top before tightening the drawstring. Kylie deftly wove a basket out of air and levitated the cumbersome bag to knee height. I admired her skill. I could have created the same elemental lift, but I would have needed a boost of extra magic from Oliver to help me. I grabbed the over-the-shoulder straps and used them like a leash to keep the bag close to us as Kylie collected her research books and we exited the café.

"Do you think Oliver will stay behind this time?" Kylie asked.

"I doubt it." *He might if I encouraged him to.* I ignored the thought. "He's not like other gargoyles. He likes to wander."

"I think he just likes to be near you," Kylie said.

"Which is the problem." Gargoyles had a symbiotic relationship with humans. They could enhance our magic, making them coveted additions to any building or home. In turn, while they bolstered a person's magic, they also fed off it. Despite being made of stone, gargoyles required a balance of the elemental energies to be healthy. I suspected it was why most gravitated toward busy public buildings and the households of full-spectrum pentacle potentials, or FSPPs, where the inhabitants all possessed powerful control over all five elements. Living with me, Oliver consumed mostly earth, and it threw his system out of whack, making him lethargic and potentially stunting his growth. As soon as I'd realized the problem, we'd started making frequent trips to public places where he could supplement his diet.

"It's not a problem," Kylie said. "You've figured out how to keep him healthy, and when he's with you, he's happy. Besides, look at it from his perspective. He's assisting Terra Haven's one and only gargoyle healer. I bet the other gargoyles are jealous."

"Ugh. That makes me sound disgustingly self-important."

Oliver released a trill loud enough to turn every head in the busy pentagon, and the sound lifted my heart. He launched from the roof, startling a flock of pigeons when he unfurled enormous stone eagle's wings from his sinuous Chinese dragon body. Oliver was a glossy orange red of almost pure carnelian, from his square muzzle and stone beard to the feathery rock tufts at the tip of his long tail. With the sun shining through his rock feathers, he looked like he was suspended on wings of fire as he dove toward us. The graceful roll of his long body through the air made it easy to forget he weighed over a hundred pounds—until he landed too hard and his stone feet clapped against the cobblestones loud enough to echo through the surrounding buildings.

"Where are we going now?" Oliver asked. His voice had deepened as he'd grown, but it still carried the undercurrent of chimes and in no way sounded like it came from a stone throat.

Here was the moment to encourage Oliver to stay. With the variety of elementals who frequented the library, it would be a good, healthy home for him. But the words stacked up in my throat, and I swallowed them.

Oliver and his four siblings had been my first gargoyle healer case, and after I'd saved them, they'd stuck around to roost on the Victorian where Kylie and I both rented rooms. However, over the last few months, the other four had begun to explore various rooftops around the city, looking for more permanent homes. I kept waiting for Oliver to follow suit, all while hoping he'd stick around a little longer. Life without him was going to be lonely.

"To the gallery and then home. Unless you have some-where else to go, Kylie," I said. I'd been pointedly avoiding looking at Kylie so she wouldn't see my guilt, but I glanced her way when she didn't respond.

Kylie had stopped a few feet behind us, eyes riveted on a whirl of tangled air hurtling through a gap in the buildings and heading straight toward her. Though it moved fast enough to blur, I recognized her signature elemental twist on the bubble of captured sound: One of Kylie's rumor scouts had found something.

She pulled her white-blond hair aside as the air cupped her ear, feeding the message privately to her. Her blue eyes lit up and a flush brightened her pale cheeks.

"Well?" I asked. "What's the story?" If anything put that glow on my journalist friend's face, it was the possibility of a front-page piece of news.

"I don't know. Maybe nothing. I've got to go."

The weave dropped from beneath my bag and it crashed to the cobblestones, jerking my shoulder with it.

"Oh, sorry. Here." Kylie thrust her books into my arms. "I'll send word if I'll be done by dinner. Bye!" She spun and sprinted toward the nearest alley, shoulder-length hair streaming behind her as she disappeared around the corner.

"Okay, then. It's just you and me, Oliver." I crouched to add Kylie's books to my bag. This wasn't the first time Kylie had literally raced away, chasing a story. If it panned out, I'd find out about it tonight or tomorrow. In the meantime, I had errands to finish and work of my own. "Unless you want to stay," I forced myself to say.

"I want to see what sold," he said.

The tightness in my chest eased as I shared a smile with the little gargoyle.

I swung one strap of the bag over my shoulder and rested the awkward, poky bulk against my left hip, leaning to the right to compensate. After two steps, I switched sides with Oliver. His long body and four stubby legs gave him a bunching, loping gate, and his back kept bumping the bottom of the bag. Perhaps *little* wasn't the right term for him anymore. He was almost three feet long and half as tall with his wings closed. When he'd first come to live with me, he'd been small enough to hold. If I didn't stunt him and he kept growing at a normal rate, he'd reach over six feet long.

"Want to make any predictions?" I asked.

"The gargoyle pendants will be sold out, of course," he said. "Especially the ones of me."

"That goes without saying." My lifelong dream of becoming Terra Haven's preeminent quartz artisan had veered off course when I'd discovered I could heal gargoyles. Now, I wouldn't change a thing, but I still enjoyed working with inert quartz, and since being a gargoyle healer provided sporadic income, I made jewelry and sold the items through a local gallery to supplement my earnings.

"Maybe the wind current earrings, too," Oliver said, eyeing the earrings I wore. I wriggled my head to set the earrings in motion, and the gargoyle's bright eyes tracked the movement.

Like all my pieces, the earrings were made out of quartz. These were carnelian—at Oliver's request—and I'd reshaped the sturdy rock to slender, twisting ribbons so light the breeze fluttered them against my neck. Maintaining the structural integrity of the quartz while stretching it so thin took a level of skill that had taken me almost a decade to master. I owed my abilities as a gargoyle healer to those years of dedication, too. I'd worn my hair up so the sun could shine through the slivers of orange rock and catch people's eyes. Since I was the only person in the city escorted everywhere by a gargoyle, I tended to attract attention, and I wasn't above trading on the free advertising.

Oliver wriggled the ruff of rock fur behind his ears, as if

he were trying to mimic the movement of my earrings. Laughing at his antics, I completely missed seeing the bundle of elemental energy barreling toward me. The outer air layer hit me like a pillow upside the head, then bounced back and expanded into an oval sheet of fire held together with traces of air and water. Heat radiated from it, and I retreated a step when the golden and red flames reshaped into the perfect likeness of a man's face. He scowled, his bright eyes blazing straight into mine.

"Mika Stillwater," he snapped. "Your services are required on an urgent matter. Come at once."

Seeing the fiery face move was disconcerting enough; hearing the burning mouth bark my name chased a thrill of alarm down my spine. I clutched the handle of my bag tighter and shifted another step back. The disembodied flaming head followed.

I'd seen long-distance projections sent with such precision before, but only as invitations to special events. Given the tension in the man's face, he wasn't summoning me to a social gathering.

I opened my mouth to respond, but he looked to the side at something only he could see, then back at me. This time his gaze rested beyond my shoulder, and I realized it was a captured message, not a projection. I also realized I knew him.

"Your specialty is needed," he growled. The sphere collapsed into an arrow of pure flame. It darted away from me, then spun and pointed left down a side street. It held that position, quivering in place.

"Wasn't that—"

"Full-spectrum guard Velasquez," I said, finishing Oliver's question. *The most powerful fire elemental I'd ever met,* I added silently. You didn't make it into the ranks of the

Federal Pentagon Defense, the country's most elite law enforcement organization, unless you were an FSPP or nearly so. I'd had the good fortune to meet the local FPD full-five squad when I'd rescued Oliver and his siblings, but I hadn't expected to encounter the specialized team again, let alone receive a personal summons from the burly fire elemental.

Velasquez's words sank past my surprise. The only reason he would need me was if a gargoyle was in trouble.

"We need to hurry," I said, yanking my backpack's straps securely over both arms.

"Someone needs us!" Oliver shouted gleefully.

The moment I lurched into motion, the flaming arrow moved. As if attached to me by a stiff tether, it kept exactly the same distance between us even as I picked up my pace to a run. Oliver loped like an enormous inchworm ahead of me, his back arching and straightening with each stride, and he unfurled his wings for short glides to increase his speed.

Watching his increasingly long leaps, I was struck by a feeling of déjà vu. It'd been a race through the streets after a baby gargoyle that had altered the course of my life. Until that moment, I'd been a rather typical earth elemental, with a stable job and a life spent mostly behind a worktable. These days, I did a lot more rushing about, usually racing toward injured gargoyles, and I didn't think I'd ever get used to this nauseating jolt of adrenaline.

Between Oliver's stone feet pounding on the cobblestones, my heavy steps, and the clatter of seed crystals knocking together in my bag, we made enough racket to sound like a rampaging minotaur. People scurried out of our way and gawked from the edges of the road. Several waved and pointed, calling out encouragement. A few actually knew my name.

Our guiding arrow took us through downtown, winding along the least crowded roads. We pounded down wide sidewalks and through narrow alleys, and every time the arrow darted out of sight, I prayed it had stopped just around the corner so I could rest. My lungs and legs burned, and the heavy sack pummeled bruises into my lower back.

I zigzagged past a tavern and a haberdashery, before the narrow street opened into Focal Park. Or it should have. I stumbled to a halt. A massive blue-green ward twice as tall as the nearest building cordoned off the mile-long public park. As far as I could see up and down the street, emergency personnel held focal points of the shimmering ward at regular intervals. I braced my hands on my knees, sucking in oxygen. I'd never seen a ward that huge. It looked like it was designed to keep out an invading army.

And Velasquez's fiery arrow pointed straight at it.

———

A crowd of people loitered outside the park's earth entrance, where guards blockaded the pathway to a tunnel hidden behind the ward. Most of the people must have been herded from the park, judging by the number of blankets, picnic baskets, and various sports equipment they held. Questions rumbled through the displaced citizens, but I didn't hear any answers.

Together Oliver and I wormed through the crowd, and as people noticed Oliver, they cleared a path.

"Is there a sick gargoyle in the park?" someone shouted.

"I've heard gargoyles go berserk. Is that what happened?" another person asked.

I shook my head at the absurd question, but I couldn't

take my eyes from the towering ward. What was Velasquez involving me in?

A woman burst through the crowd and grabbed my arm, and I yelped before recognizing Kylie.

"What's that?" she asked, pointing to the burning arrow hovering just this side of the ward. It'd received some nervous looks from the crowd and a few from the guards, too.

"Don't scare me like that," I said. "It's a summons from Velasquez." Kylie knew who the fire elemental was without me needing to remind her. She'd been there when the full-five squad had carted away the man who'd kidnapped Oliver and his siblings. Since then, she'd followed the squad more than once for a story. In fact . . . "Was your rumor scout about the captain?"

Flushing, Kylie crossed her arms defensively. "Yes."

My stomach sank. Kylie had a standing rumor scout patrolling for mention of Captain Grant Monaghan, the air elemental in charge of Velasquez's squad. If the captain was here, the whole squad probably was, which meant the danger level of whatever I was rushing toward was far greater than a sick gargoyle. The ward more than confirmed it.

"What did he say?" Kylie asked.

"He needs me."

Kylie's eyebrows shot upward. "That's what Mr. Gruffy-Pants himself said?"

"Basically." My footsteps had slowed while I talked, and Oliver butted my palm with a soft whine. The same urgency hummed in my veins, but I couldn't have Kylie following us into danger.

"Wait here," I told Kylie. "I'll tell you everything later.

It'll be an exclusive." I winked, then spun toward the tunnel entrance.

"Really? You thought that'd work?" Kylie fell into step on the other side of Oliver. "The people have a right to know what's going on in there, and if Grant is in there, I need to make sure he—ah, that the squad—is okay and . . . acting in the best interest of the citizens. A government that keeps secrets from the people is a corrupt government."

Her slipup was more telling than her ongoing protests about democracy and the balancing power of the press.

"Fine," I hissed as we approached the guards posted at the park entrance. The burning arrow hadn't moved from where it pressed an inch away from the ward, crushing my meager hope that Velasquez stood on this side of the ward.

"The park is closed," a tall woman in uniform said.

"I see that," I said, and Kylie snorted, then turned the sound into a cough. The guard scowled at us both. "I was summoned by FPD Fire Elemental Velasquez." I pointed to the arrow. "I'm a gargoyle healer, and he said I'm needed." I added a point toward Oliver, in case she'd missed the presence of the excited stone dragon who pranced between Kylie and me.

"And I'm her assistant," Kylie said. I wanted to protest, but I knew how much her career meant to her, and there was obviously a story on the other side of this magical curtain. Plus I was beginning to suspect her crush on Captain Monaghan might have developed into something more, so I kept my mouth shut and tried not to fidget.

The guard looped a bubble of air around the burning arrow and yanked it to us. She probed the elemental strands, and the message unfurled again. Velasquez's hard expression glared at the guard this time as he called me to his side without a single *please* or an ounce of deference in his tone.

When the message reverted to an arrow of flame, the guard released it and gestured for her companions to let us pass. Oliver trundled ahead with Kylie close beside him, but my footsteps lagged. As long as I remained on this side of the ward, I was safe.

But a gargoyle wasn't.

I hurried to catch up with Kylie and Oliver.

ABOUT THE AUTHOR

REBECCA CHASTAIN is the *USA Today* bestselling author of the Madison Fox urban fantasy series and the Gargoyle Guardian Chronicles fantasy trilogy, among other works. Inside her novels, you'll find spellbinding adventures packed with supernatural creatures, thrilling action, heart-warming characters (human and otherwise), and more than a little humor. She lives in Northern California with her wonderful husband and three bossy cats.

Unlock bonus content:
Visit RebeccaChastain.com
for extras, giveaways, and so much more!

Join Rebecca on Facebook and Twitter
facebook.com/rebeccachastainnovels
@Author_Rebecca

FROM *USA TODAY*
BESTSELLING AUTHOR

REBECCA CHASTAIN

Madison's new job would be perfect,
if not for all the creatures trying to
eat her soul...

A FISTFUL OF EVIL
A FISTFUL OF FIRE
A FISTFUL OF FROST

PRAISE FOR THE MADISON FOX NOVELS

"Rebecca Chastain has a hit series here,
one full of humor, danger and amazingly
awesome characters!"
–*Tome Tender*

"a masterfully plotted urban fantasy... I highly
recommend it to readers of all ilk, urban fantasy
aficionados, or not."
–*Open Book Society*

"a great mixture of action, danger, fantasy,
and humor"
–*Books That Hook*

RebeccaChastain.com